Climb On!

Success Strategies for Teens

JOHN BEEDE

To book the author for speaking engagements at student
leadership conferences, school assemblies, or other events,
please visit www.climbonsuccess.com for information.

CLIMB ON!
Success Strategies for Teens

John Beede

Copyright © 2005, 2008, 2009, 2012 John Beede

Published by:
Sierra Nevada Publishing House
PO Box 232395
Las Vegas, NV 89105
1-800-CLIMB-ON
john@climbonsuccess.com

Originally printed as:
Climb On! Dynamic Strategies for Teen Success

Printed in the United States of America

Edited by Elizabeth (Rubie) Gosnell.
Cover design and layout: Ad Graphics, Inc., Tulsa, OK.
Equipment images courtesy Metolius Climbing,
Blue Water Ropes, La Sportiva Shoes, and Petzl.
Used with permission.

LCCN: 2005904531

ISBN: 978-0-9765697-0-1

The Author Welcomes
Correspondence From Readers!

* * * * *

Speaker, author, and adventurer John Beede has been professionally speaking at leadership and school events all over the US and Canada for over 10 years. Still in his mid-twenties, he uses his unique, one-of-a-kind worldwide adventures as a metaphor for personal success.

**To inquire about booking John to speak
at your next event, please contact;**

1-800-CLIMB-ON (1-800-254-6266)
john@climbonsuccess.com
www.climbonsuccess.com

John also loves hearing from his readers and audience members. If you have a non-speaking related inquiry comment, or compliment, feel free to write or email. John personally responds to every contact, however, it may take him a few days due to his busy schedule.

Special Surprise Bonus for Readers Like YOU!

For more than

$97

in additional resources from the author, please visit:

www.climbonsuccess.com/freegift

What Others Are Saying About CLIMB ON!

* * * * *

"A wonderfully simple approach to success. This book is fun, user friendly, and the perfect kick-in-the-butt when you need it most."

Sean Covey
Author of the International Bestseller
The Seven Habits of Highly Effective Teens

"John Beede was probably one of the most inspiring, energetic, and passionate speakers out there today! I heard him speak at the National Student Council Conference, and I was very much changed. He taught me that no matter what circumstance you are in, you have the choice to *Climb On!* and make the most of it all."

JR Planas
Las Vegas, NV

"Packed with amazing stories, fun characters, and great lessons, this book could make every teen in America a *Soul Surfer* in their own right."

Bethany Hamilton
Author, *Soul Surfer*
ESPY Comeback Athlete of the Year
Teen Choice Award for "Courage"

"The ideas and concepts presented in *Climb On!* represent in a nut shell everything I talk about in my speeches across the country. I always say 'aim high and dream big,' now I will be adding '*Climb On!*'"

Troy McClain
The Apprentice Season 1 Contestant
The Home Team Host

"*Climb On!* is simple, but it packs a punch that can dramatically change your life for the better. John has led an unusually successful life for his young age and in this book, he lays out exactly how you can do the **same for yourself! Read it!**"

Rudy Ruettiger
Inspiration for TriStar Pictures Movie Rudy
Notre Dame Football Hero

"These exciting ideas will help you climb to the greatest heights in your life."

Brian Tracy
Personal and Business Success Superstar

"Climb On! is a great blueprint for any student who wants to make something of themselves. Read it! I give it a 10!"

Peter Vidmar
Olympic Gymnastics Gold Medallist

"A wonderful story with keen insight not only into the struggles teens share in today's world, but also their true desire to achieve more in their lives. An easy, powerful read for teens, and an important read for all who work with, parent, and care about our most important commodity in the world ñ the youth of today."

Joe Gandolpho
"America's DADvocate"
Professional Speaker, Licensed Professional Counselor

"*Climb On!* is an easy-to-read, fun guideline that teaches young people that they have the power to choose the kind of lives they will live, and that they alone are responsible for making that choice a good one. It is a 'must-read' for every young person… and equally beneficial for adults!"

Ed Foreman
Former Congressman of two states, New Mexico and Texas

"I loved the whole book. I just wish there was more to read!"

Rose Thelen
8th Grade Student

"*Climb On!* What a great metaphor for perseverance, one of my keys to success. Your book is exciting and poignant. A wonderful story for youth audiences to read and learn from. Every reader will take away something from this book."

Lloyd H. Bachrach
Yes, You Can! Inc.
1996 USA Paralympian

"His work came at ironically the perfect time… it feels like a sign of relief has come to me. It was wonderful. Designed as if for me."

Deaudre LeCato
12th Grade Student

"*Climb On!* cuts to the chase in what matters in life; that we figure out what we want and move towards making it happen. John's laid it all out for you, in a process you can begin today!"

Warren Macdonald
Spreaker, Adventurer, Author of *A Test of Will*

"A fun book with great lessons for all of us. If you want to know what it takes to achieve success in your life, you have to read this!"

Gareth Wood
First Unsupported 900 mile trek to South Pole
"One of the ten greatest feats of the decade"... *Outside* **Magazine**

"As a fighter, I learned what it takes to succeed the hard way, but you don't have to. *Climb On!* is an incredible book, but more importantly, it's a road map for creating the life you want. Read and apply these principals and you'll immediately start getting more of what you want and being the person you came on this planet to be. There is no greater measure of success!"

Don Akers
Olympic Boxing Contender, Author, Professional Speaker

"John Beede has written a book that will grab teenage readers and their parents. Through the medium of rock climbing, high schoolers learn to confront issues with parents, teachers, and each other. Very readable and keeps your attention to the end. You watch the teens grow strong and confident as they conquer the rocks and at the same time conquer their fears."

Emily Kimball
The Aging Adventurer
Make It Happen!

"If every teenager in America had to read and apply the lessons of *Climb On!* before they finished school, our country would no longer have problems with teen drug abuse, suicide, or pregnancy. And as a side benefit, John Beede would be fabulously wealthy."

Joshua Sundquist
Co-author of *Forty Voices: Stories of Hope from Our Generation*

"If you are going for the gold in life, *Climb On!* is a must-read."

Ruben Gonzalez
Olympian, Author, Keynote Speaker

"Bravo! Mr. Beede nailed it! Excellent stories coupled with awesome strategies for teen success. This book eliminates the question, 'How do I succeed as a teen?' A must-read for teens and pre-teens."

Kevin Bracy
America's Best at Connecting With Generation Next
#1 Speaker for Monster.com's MIC Programs 6 Years in a Row

"People complain about the poor state of teens today. John has stepped up to the plate and is doing something about it... and what he's doing is working. His life is clearly dedicated to the improvement of others."

Kevin Palau
Exec. VP, PalauFest Productions

"I enjoyed every moment of reading and doing the applications of *Climb On!* I believe that your book will help all teens. Many kids graduate not knowing what they want and this book will help them to be successful."

Savanah McQuiston
7th Grade Student

"*Climb On!* is a great blueprint for any teen who wants to turn themselves into something great. Read it! I give it a 10!"

Mike Schlappi
Four-Time Olympic Medallist

"A wonderfully simple approach to success. Everyone, teens and adults alike will benefit from the lessons in *Climb On!*"

Beth Rodden & Tommy Caldwell
First free ascent of El Capitan's "Lurking Fear" (5.13a).
Beth holds world record for hardest first female ascent (5.14b).

"*Climb On!* Helps both teens and adults alike achieve their goals. Way to go, John!"

Jill Spiegel
Author, speaker, and president of Goal Getters.
Host of The Jill Spiegel Show.

"Thank you for the opportunity you gave us students to have confidence in ourselves. There is a little bit of everything in this book. Romance lessons, humor, smart-alecky remarks, and much more."

Rebekah Ewing
7th Grade Student

"Oh man I don't even know how to say how much I loved your speech.... :) First of all, your enthusiasm was the best! You connected soo well with everyone and you kept me interested! You talked about things teenagers can relate to, and we appreciate that so much! You have no idea. Your stories were inspirational and I had an overall incredible time listening to you!!"

Morgan Illa
Student, Overton Park, KS

This book is dedicated to my grandfather.
He was my favorite storyteller.

CONTENTS

* * * * *

INTRODUCTION

A True Story

I am convinced I will die within seconds. My cracked and chapped fingertips are caked with blood. My muscles are twitching from lactic acid build up. Grime is smeared across my ruddy face.

A bead of sweat forms on my forehead and slithers its way down to the tip of my nose. It hangs for a moment. And falls. And falls. Until I lose sight of it. The only thing preventing me from slamming into the jagged rocks below me is three hundred feet… of air.

I'm rock climbing in Leavenworth, nestled in Eastern Washington State's mountain range. Gregg, my climbing partner and I have been climbing since sunrise and have had no problems. So we took a risk.

"Look, the first bolt is right there. I can climb out to it," I persuaded Gregg, minutes before I found myself pinned. "When I get to it, we'll be fine. Piece of cake."

It wasn't a piece of cake. The rock was deceptively barren of handholds. I clumsily traversed the cliff face and ended up with nowhere to go... but down. The bolt that would save my life, if I could get to it, was about two feet above my reach. My arms twitched from exhaustion. I looked at Gregg. He knew I was in trouble. Our rope was tied between us. If I fell, he would fall with me. He knew he was in trouble.

My palms slapped in vain against the rock, searching for a handhold. Nothing. "Slipping!"

"Hang in there John." Gregg said, fearfully.

"I can't. It's impossible."

"John?"

"Yeah?"

Gregg said two powerful words that probably saved our lives.

"Climb on!"

That's where the title for this book comes from. In these pages are proven guidelines to help you do... well... anything you want. Really! You name it. Grades, sports, boyfriends, girlfriends, work, clubs, whatever. You have enough people telling you what to do, how to do it, and that you should do things differently. If you put to use what you'll find in the pages you are holding, you can get what *you* want out of life.

You'll find this book to be unique. It is a story that teaches lessons, also known as a parable. The book is packed with action, quirky characters, and a touch of romance. It's a fun read, but you will have missed the point if you don't learn the lessons as well. So, when you read, imagine yourself to be the main character learning the same lessons that she does. You'll get more out of it that way. Also, do the exercises. In fact, if you follow the strategies you'll find in this book, do the exercises, and still don't get to where you want to go, I'll mail you back your money for this book. That's how confident I am in these principles.

So what happened on the rock?

There's a move in the climbing world known as a "dyno." It is an extremely dangerous move. Using whatever handhold or foothold a climber can find, he or she hurtles off of the rock and leaps into the air to grab an out-of-reach handhold. I knew it was what I had to do.

"I'll count to three," I told Gregg. "One…" I secure my feet and pinch my dime-sized finger hold. "Two…" Life or death decision for two people. "Three…" Launch! I float in slow motion through the air. My arms stretch like rubber bands for the handhold next to the bolt. Closer. Closer. Pow! My left hand locks onto the rock like the jaws of a tiger. My left foot scuffles to find a quick foothold. With my free hand I grab a clip off of my harness, attach it to the rope and then to the bolt.

I did it. I was safe.

Will you dyno with me? Will you stretch yourself to achieve what you may believe to be impossible? I'll say to you the same thing Gregg said to me. *Climb On!*

– John Beede

CHAPTER ONE

Las Vegas – Early March

"Hey, darlin'! What's happening?" Anna jumped at the voice that came from behind her, nearly slipping off the roof. "I'm Jeremy. Good to meetchya!" He grinned like a goblin, his hands on his hips, proud of scaring Anna.

"How'd you get up here?" Anna asked, startled. Her hands clutched the roofing shingles behind her.

"Up the side of the house," Jeremy said with a smile.

"The side of the house? Who are you—Spider-man?" Anna raised an eyebrow at the intruder. Despite her initial fear, she had to admit that he had a cute smile. The moon's white light glowed on Jeremy's wavy blonde hair and big blue eyes. Both gave him an innocent look. He was about Anna's age, around 16.

"Yeah, the bricks make for good finger holds. Sorry, didn't mean to scare you."

"So you just...climbed up the side of my house?" Anna asked in disbelief. She was up there to get away; her room's balcony was perfectly positioned for her to climb up on her roof. Granted, shingles aren't particularly comfortable to sit on, but they were a better trade-off than dealing with life in the house below.

"Yep," said Jeremy with a straight face. "Getting past the rain gutter without breaking it was a little tough, but other than that, it was a good climb."

"You must have set up a ladder or something."

"Nope." Jeremy was straight-faced.

"Wait, who are you and why did you climb up the side of my house?"

"Oh, sorry to weird you out. I'm Jeremy. I live down the street a ways. Just got back from practice, saw you up here, and couldn't help but wonder, 'Now what's a pretty girl like that doing on her roof?' Thought you'd like some company. Should I leave?"

Anna's shoulder length auburn hair fluttered in the wind a bit. "I'll push you when I want you to leave."

"Whoa there, feisty. What's your name?" Her hostility didn't phase Jeremy. He invited himself to a seat next to her, checking out the view.

"Anna." She flipped up her vest collar to block the early March wind. Her dark brown eyes seemed to pierce the sky.

"Anna what?"

"Anna Anna. OK?"

"Parents aren't very original are they?" Jeremy joked. "Well, Anna Anna, I'm Jeremy Fuller." He stuck out his hand. She ignored it. "So what's the deal? Why are you on the roof?"

Anna stared out at the city; the glow of the distant casino lights gave the growing thunderclouds an eerie look. In her mind, she replayed the fight she had just had with her dad. One of those stupid fights over nothing worth fighting over. He accused Anna of breaking some of the glasses in the dishwasher. *How was I supposed to know the glasses would crack if I lined them all up next to each other? Besides, it's dumb to yell at me for what I did accidentally.* She really didn't want to share her family life with this rooftop-mounting stranger. "You like Vegas?" she asked.

"I like this town just about as much as you like avoiding the subject."

"You're almost as rude as me," Anna said.

"That's why we'll make such good friends."

Is this guy starved for attention or what? Well... I guess he's just trying to be nice.

"I'm sorry. Anna May Keller's my name. I'm just ticked off."

"Well, I don't want to ruin my rude streak and not intrude. So, care to share?"

She had a faint urge to tell Jeremy all she had been

thinking about. Anna compared herself to the city of Las Vegas: at school, she put on the nice and glitzy act, just like the upscale hotels do. But her friendships felt hollow... she wouldn't even call them friends. Just acquaintances. Just like Las Vegas has a nasty underbelly with drugs, gangs, and prostitution, Anna felt like she had to keep her darker, depressed side hidden. She choked back a knot in her throat.

"I don't want to get into it. My life's a mess." Anna looked straight into Jeremy's eyes, "You're the one climbing walls, but I feel like I'm Spiderman, you know, leading two lives."

"C'mon now, Peter Parker, what's so bad about your life?"

"Peter Parker?" She gave up a quick smirk. "Cute." From her pocket, Anna pulled the unsatisfactory grade notice she had plucked out of the mail earlier that day. She eyed it with a touch of disdain and handed it to Jeremy.

"Hey, you go to the same school as me," Jeremy noted, looking at the report.

"Wish I didn't."

He teased her, "You wish you didn't go to the same school as me? You don't even know me yet."

"No, dork, I wish I didn't go to *that* school. And what makes you think there's a 'yet?'"

"A guy can hope can't he? Anyway, what's so bad about school?"

"Until two years ago, I lived in a picket-fence community in a Colorado suburb. Life was good. Friends. Grades. Family was fine…"

There was a pause.

"Then?" Jeremy prodded.

"Nothing." She insisted, but it wasn't nothing. Anna knew what she would say if she knew this guy. Something like:

Then mom started drinking. OK? She wouldn't stop. I came home from school and she'd be there, drunk on the couch. She'd yell or cuss at my little brother and me.

"You sure you don't want to talk?" Jeremy asked.

"Nothing to say." But there was.

We tried getting her to Alcoholics Anonymous meetings, pleading, fighting, yelling, whatever. One night she hit my little brother, Charlie. That was the last straw for my dad, so they got a divorce.

The events happened so quickly that Anna hadn't had time to process what was happening. Before she knew it, her dad had a job transfer to Las Vegas, and she and Charlie were unpacking a U-Haul at their new home. That was almost a year ago now.

"You're sure?" Jeremy asked once more.

Anna snapped, mostly just wanting to stop the interrogation. "Listen kid, first it was my mom, dad, brother, and I. We were together. A family. Then there was the divorce, and it was just my dad, brother, and me. Now what? It's just me! My brother and dad do their own thing. My mom is halfway across the country, and I'm left alone! At school, I'm just a number on some bald guy's chart. Nobody cares. This whole town's a disgusting dump and so is life! Are you happy now?" Anna dropped her face into her hands and cried.

Those last words hung in the air. *Disgusting dump.* Jeremy put his hand on Anna's shoulder. She brushed it away.

After an uncomfortable pause, Anna rubbed the tears from her eyes and tried to change the subject. "Sorry. Anyway, you said you just got back from practice. What do you play?"

Jeremy's mind shifted gears, "Oh, right. I'm on a rock climbing team."

Anna sat up straighter. "That doesn't seem like a team sport to me."

"We're a team because our lives depend on each other. I mean, if someone isn't paying attention, then…" Jeremy smacked his hand against the rooftop, pretending it was a climber falling to the ground.

"I get the picture." Anna had to admit he was a little bizarre. "You climb at night?"

Jeremy clarified, "There's an indoor climbing gym a few miles up the road. You know, with holds bolted into the wall and stuff. And lights," he added, smiling.

During their conversation, the clouds from the distant thunderstorm moved overhead and a drizzle began. When it rains in Las Vegas, it pours, so Jeremy and Anna decided to call it a night.

"Well, thanks for climbing onto my roof I guess," Anna said.

"My pleasure," Jeremy beamed. "Hey, I was thinking. How do you get to school in the morning?"

"The bus."

Jeremy stood and bowed as though Anna were royalty. "Does your majesty need a ride to school tomorrow?"

She thought for a few seconds. "Beats the bus. Talk about a disgusting dump! Where should I meet you?"

"Be outside at 6:30."

"Sure, see ya then. Thanks."

Jeremy walked to the side of the roof, spun around, and holding onto the edge, he disappeared just as quickly as he appeared. Anna turned up one side of her mouth in amazement.

The smile morphed to a frown when she thought about the day on the horizon. School. In the educational institution that Anna considered a prison, she felt more like cattle than a person. Herded into class, herded out. Five minutes between classes to get to the next room. Twenty-five minutes for lunch. Hall monitors ranching kids into windowless rooms. Words like *cold, impersonal, dreary, gray, bland,* and *dull* came to mind when she thought of her daily routine. She looked up to the sky. *It's gotta get better than this…somehow.*

She eased down to her balcony and went inside.

CHAPTER TWO

Palm Valley High School – Friday

Jeremy was already waiting in his yellow jeep as Anna stepped out the door at 6:28AM. The sun would creep over the mountains within the next half hour. Anna dragged herself down the steps to the car. "No human should be awake if the sun's not awake."

"I wholeheartedly concur." He honked his car horn for emphasis.

She had forgotten how eccentric he was.

School was the same as every other day. The usual group of students lounged in the empty desert lot across from the school, getting their morning buzz from cigarettes, some from pot. The early bird marching band was finishing up on the football field. The smell of the nearby sewers crept into Anna's nostrils. Schools in Las Vegas are sometimes built on inexpensive property, and if that means a sewer smell, then such is the cost of education.

The day didn't get any better than the sewer stink. Quarter grades were posted in Anna's first period Chemistry class. *D+? Awhh! My dad's gonna kill me! Everything's going wrong. My family's torn apart. My grades are horrible. This school smells like my grandpa's armpits...* She slumped into her chair and tried to take notes as her teacher scribbled on the board, but she mostly watched the clock. *Granite decomposes faster than this clock moves.*

She darted out of the room as soon as the bell rang. Filled with disgust at the class, she hurtled her chemistry book into her locker, wishing she'd never see it again.

Right after she slammed her locker, Anna cringed at the sound of cussing and crunching metal from behind her. Whipping around, she saw a student with long black hair and dark clothes forced against a locker. She could only see the back of the attacker's head. The gigantic assailant clenched his prey's leather jacket with both hands and slammed him into the lockers like a gorilla would toss a rag doll. More cussing. A crowd formed. Punches. Anna's jaw hung from her face as if fishing line held it on. Blood spilt on the floor. She stood there, stunned.

As quickly as the dark-haired student was attacked, he lifted his foot and pummeled his opponent in the chest. Steel-toed boots. The big guy staggered backwards and fell onto Anna. They both collapsed to the ground and Anna's head barely missed getting cracked open on the lockers. "Get off me, moron!" Before she knew it, campus police and hall monitors peeled her off the ground and half-dragged, half-helped Anna into the office along with the two fighters.

* * * * *

Mr. Tucker

"Anna?" It was a solid voice. Anna raised her head. She had been in the waiting room for the last half hour.

"Yes?"

"I'm Mr. Tucker. I helped you get checked into your classes when you first moved here." He had a look of concern on his face as he sipped his coffee. Clean cut, thin framed glasses. Well built for a high school counselor. Tall. His coffee mug had the school mascot on it and his sweatshirt had the school initials, "PV," embroidered on the breast.

Geez, this guy probably has Palm Valley toothpaste.

"Yeah, I remember you," she said.

"You doing OK?"

No sense in lying about it, she figured. "No."

"Want to come into my office to talk?"

"Not really." She stood to go with him anyway.

CLIMB ON!

He walked her down the hall to his cramped, cluttered office. There was a poster of Mt. Everest with a motivational quote at the bottom and one of a ropeless climber hanging from a cliff. "Weird," Anna said. "I met a guy yesterday who likes climbing too. Jeremy's his name. Kind of a weird guy." "Oh, you know Jeremy? He's a good climber. He used to be an arrogant little punk, but we've fixed him up pretty good." Mr. Tucker had a slight smile. Light beamed through the school's industrial shutters, shining on the dust in the air.

Anna gestured at the poster of the climber, "Is that you?"

Mr. Tucker chuckled. "No, no. I'm not insane. This is me." He pointed to a framed picture of himself on an impressively tall cliff. He had a rope. "Not all rock climbers are crazy, you know."

"Could have fooled me," Anna muttered as she sat down, not quite sure what she was supposed to tell him. Mr. Tucker grabbed a stress ball and squeezed it like he was kneading bread. He seemed like a typical gung-ho, dedicated school teacher with a hobby that happened to be cool.

"Tell me about Jeremy," he said.

Talking about Jeremy's visit last night led them to talking about why she was on the roof, which turned into a conversation about the divorce and the move, which led to talking about the fight by the lockers. Mr. Tucker just let Anna say what she wanted, asking a few questions along the way. He soon realized she had nothing to do with the fight.

Mr. Tucker had deep brown eyes with a look like they were penetrating to the depths of Anna's soul. They assured her that he actually cared about what she was saying. For a moment, she felt…safe.

I guess this guy's not too bad. "I just don't understand it, you know?" she said, "I don't get why those two guys would want to beat each other's faces in like that. I don't get a lot of things. I mean, does it get any better than this? Is it just, 'life sucks, then you die'?"

Mr. Tucker took a moment before answering. "Anna, I promise you there is enough beauty and goodness in this world to overwhelm any breathing soul. As you're finding out, however, there is also a great deal of pain and grief." He looked her in the eye for his last sentence. "The trick, Anna, is to know how to act, and not react to what happens to you."

Anna crawled back into her shell. "Not react? If a 200 pound lug nut gets kicked on top of me, of course I'm going to react to that."

"Sure. I agree. That was completely out of your control. But how you deal with what happens to you is in your control. You got pretty upset and probably still are. That's a reaction that is in your control.

From what you've told me, you're upset about living in this city, your grades, your parents, and you're livid about what just happened out there. While you didn't choose to move here, or choose for your parents to get a divorce, or choose for Muscle Ears to fall on top of you, you do choose how you deal with all those things."

"What do you mean?" Anna wasn't convinced.

Mr. Tucker got straight to making his point. "There's a student at this school who is HIV positive."

Anna was jarred by the statement. "Oh my gosh."

"This person was thrown into some poor circumstances, made some even worse decisions, and is paying for it. I'm not going to tell you who it is to protect them, but I can say that I'm this student's counselor so we've had a lot of pretty intense conversations. I got a note one day, out of the blue, about how this disease has changed this person's life. Later, I received permission to read a part of this letter to other students who I think it'd help. Mind if I read it?"

"Uh, OK."

Mr. Tucker pulled the letter out of a file cabinet, adjusted his glasses, and cleared his throat,

"At first, I went through a long depression. I mean, I was completely shell shocked for almost half a year. Everything seemed so pointless. I was handed a death sentence. For months, I was like, 'Why would I want to do anything knowing I'm just going to die?' After I thought about what we've talked about for a LONG time, I realized my disease is only a reminder of how special life is and how much I need to value what I've got and what's in the world. It's kinda weird how happy I feel. I mean, today I caught myself staring at a bike rack, thinking how beautiful it was. What's up with that, right? But I don't want it any other way. I mean, I appreciate life so much more than everyone else and I really think I'm happier than they are too."

Mr. Tucker put the letter away and pulled off his glasses. "Anna, that's what I mean by acting and not reacting to what happens to you. The student is in a terrible situation and has chosen to be happy."

"I guess I can see that." The story touched her, but she also thought Mr. Tucker was starting to sound like a late-night cable TV motivational special.

"I probably shouldn't tell you this, but there's a teacher here that not many of us like because she's so negative all the time. A real she-devil. Well, a few weeks ago, this teacher went out gambling and won 6,000 dollars."

Anna raised her eyebrows. She didn't know if she was surprised at the amount the teacher won or at the fact that a teacher went somewhere besides school.

"Yeah. Pretty wild. She was excited for about a week, then she slipped back into her negative, nasty attitude. Do you see the difference between the teacher and the student?"

Anna said what she thought he wanted to hear. "The student had something bad happen and saw the good in it, right?"

"Right." Mr. Tucker said. "And the teacher had something good happen and continued being miserable. This tells me it's not what happens to people that makes them happy or sad. It's how they choose to feel, in spite of the things that happen. See what I'm saying?"

"I guess."

"Listen, I know school can feel really cold and impersonal sometimes. But really, that's your problem. You can mope and whine and complain, or you can choose to be happy."

"You're probably going to say the same thing about my parents and grades, aren't you?"

"Precisely. And the fight that landed you on the floor. It's not so much what happens that matters, but what you do about it that really counts."

"OK, well, good talking with you. Could I get a pass back to class?" Anna snatched the pass and was out of there before Mr. Tucker had a chance to finish writing it.

* * * * *

Smoothies – Friday Afternoon

After school, Jeremy and Anna met at his yellow jeep.

"Hiya gorgeous!" Jeremy said. "How was your day?"

"Painful."

"Let me buy you a smoothie?"

"Let's do it."

He revved the engine and they took off to Jamba Juice. They watched people and traffic pass by, and talked about each other's days. Soon, they were laughing like old friends. Jeremy couldn't help but eye Anna. She was something special. She caught him staring.

"Do I have a raspberry seed stuck in my teeth?" Anna asked, smiling and biting her straw. She knew there was nothing in her teeth.

"Uh, duh, oh, sorry. No, nothing."

Anna giggled at Jeremy's clumsiness. "You really know how to woo a girl with your words, don't you?" He could climb her roof but stuttered over smoothies. *How cute.* She decided to push it. "You think I'm cute?"

Jeremy was getting uncomfortable. That only encouraged Anna.

Anna nudged him with her elbow. "Come on, just admit it."

"Nope."

"Oh, come on," she nudged him again, smiling. "Just whisper it to me. Say you think I'm cute."

"How can I resist that smile? OK, but you have to promise not to tell anyone I told you."

Anna nodded her head in approval. Jeremy leaned closer towards her ear and said, "*BURP!*"

"Gross!" Anna said.

Jeremy thought his poor manners were uproariously funny. Anna didn't share his sentiments. "You know, you would be kind of charming if your personality didn't get in the way," she joked.

"Ha ha," his chuckles simmered down. "Yeah, but what fun would life be then?"

"You're a pig."

"You said I'm charming."

"I said you would be if you weren't a jerk." She punched his shoulder.

"Well, this jerk wants to know if you'd like to go rock climbing with him tomorrow." Jeremy said.

"You want me to go climbing with you? Just like that?" Anna was caught off guard.

"Yeah. I do. There's a big group of us that goes every weekend. Come on, you'll love it."

"I've never been."

"So?"

"So I won't know what to do. I'll look like an idiot."

"Want to hear a story?" Jeremy asked.

"Sure."

Jeremy paused a moment to think and began. "Once there was a little princess who lived in a tower. Then a big strong knight came to rescue her. She said, 'I'm not leaving with you. I've never been outside the tower.' So the knight left and she lived in the tower forever and died. The end."

"What kind of sick story is that?" Anna asked.

"That's the story that just convinced you to come climbing with me tomorrow."

She realized he had a point. "Fine. I'll go with you."

Jeremy smiled. "Great. Wear some pants or shorts you can maneuver in and make sure to ask your dad."

CHAPTER THREE

Red Rock Canyon
Saturday Morning

After a 40-minute drive the next morning, the Las Vegas city architecture abruptly ended and they were on a one-lane road surrounded by Joshua trees and cacti. Brown mountains speckled the landscape. Just as many cyclists and runners were on the road as cars. Jeremy suddenly took a sharp right turn. Anna wouldn't even have seen the street if he hadn't turned onto it.

"Welcome to Red Rock, my dear!" Jeremy's eyes glowed as he looked at the fiery red boulders and cliffs that appeared to burst from the sandy ground like fresh flames from a campfire.

Red Rock Canyon. Huge mountains of deep red and occasional cream streaks stood majestically and proudly, and judging by her expressions, they struck awe into Anna. Jeremy stopped at a booth to pay the park fee and the attendant gave them a brochure. "The park gets more than a million visitors each year," it said. The attraction was apparent. The mountains were several thousand feet of sheer vertical cliff; the canyon geology looked like solidified ooze painted red.

"This is unbelievable!" Anna's jaw hung in amazement.

"I know. Smell the air." He closed his eyes and took a deep breath.

"Eyes on the road there, champ!" Anna grabbed the wheel.

"Oh, sorry. My bad." Jeremy smiled. "Guess we couldn't teach you to *Climb On!* if you were stuck in a cactus on the side of the road." Jeremy joked.

"*Climb On!*? What do you mean?"

"You don't know what *Climb On!* is? Mr. Tucker said you guys talked."

"Mr. Tucker? What does he have to do with this?"

"Well, he's climbing with us today, for starters."

"You're kidding."

"About what?"

"Mr. Tucker. He's not coming climbing." Anna was almost annoyed.

"Well, yeah. He's probably there already." Jeremy looked at his watch. "He's the one who taught me how to climb."

"Unbelievable."

"Anna, he's a really cool guy. I figured he'd have taught you one of the *Climb On!* lessons already."

"He gave me some motivational garbage about choosing my attitude."

"Garbage? His stuff is great. Did you listen to what he said?"

"We talked. But, whatever, I can't believe I'm going climbing with my school counselor."

"Get over it. I mean, give him a chance. You'll like him. Promise. He'll teach you this philosophy. It's really a good thing."

"Teaching? Philosophy? It's like I'm going to school on a Saturday. So, wait, these *Climb On!* lessons, or whatever. You've been saying that. What's that all about?"

"It's what we call a set of lessons, our strategies for success. They teach you how to do whatever you want, really.

"That doesn't sound too bad."

"It's not. You're going to love it. *Climb On!* is a simple concept, but powerful. And it works. Like Mr. Tucker says, 'It doesn't take a complicated idea to change your life for the better. It takes a simple idea that you decide to apply to yourself. The world is complicated. A simple solution… is the solution.'" Jeremy did his best at impersonating the counselor.

"So whatever I want to do, this'll teach me how to do it. And it's easy."

"Pretty much," said Jeremy as he passed a car. "There are actually three adults who will be here. Mr. Tucker is one, there's Tommy Edgely, and Doc McAllister."

"Is this a cult?"

Jeremy laughed out loud. "No, this isn't a cult. Listen, the other night you said you wanted your life to get better. These guys will help you with that if you give 'em a chance."

"You've got a lot of nerve bringing me out here not telling me all this first."

"Anna, you're cute when you're angry, you know that?"

"Don't change the subject," Anna said.

"Listen," Jeremy persuaded, "While you're out here, you might as well give these lessons a chance."

"Why's that?"

"'Cuz we're here."

The car zoomed into a parking lot where a group of about a nine people waited. The red cliffs acted as their backdrop. Mr. Tucker was there, smiling. A pony-tailed brunette woman in her early thirties stood beside him with her hands on her hips. Anna guessed she was Doc McAllister. Several students Anna's age surrounded a man in his mid-twenties with dreadlocked, long blonde hair and a bunch of piercings, including a bar through his eyebrow.

"That's Tommy Edgely," Jeremy pointed out as they hopped out of the car and walked towards the group. We all just call him Edgely, though.

Anna did a double take, confirming his multiple piercings and dreadlocked hair.

"He's a stuntman at one of the shows on the strip. One of the coolest guys I know. He's even been in a few movies." Jeremy smiled in admiration. They were greeted with a flurry of cheers and hellos from the group. Mr. Tucker greeted her with a high-five.

Edgely stood with a large white smile and a glimmer in his eyes...or was it the glimmer off of his eyebrow piercing?

"Anna, I like you already!" Edgely said to her.

"Jeremy told me about those slobbery nut-cases at your school who fell on you." A few people snickered at his name-calling. "But you dealt with it well. I like that." Anna blushed and scuffed her foot against the ground. "I can see you're humble too. You're all right, girl." He raised his voice to address the whole group. "Today we're going to the Magic Bus Wall." There were a few groans from the group and a couple of cheers.

"That's a weird name for a cliff, isn't it?" Anna asked.

"Climbers are weird people, if you haven't noticed, Anna," Jeremy said.

Everyone picked up a bag of gear. Doc McAllister tossed Anna a rope and a water jug at the same time; Anna fumbled both and they dropped to the ground.

"Time to start carrying your share of gear, honey!" She had a thick English accent.

"OK, Doc. Nice accent by the way," said Anna as she picked the rope and jug off the ground.

"Cheers," said Doc as they started towards the trail-head.

CHAPTER FOUR

The Magic Bus Wall – Saturday Morning

After a 20-minute hike that weaved in and out of boulders the size of small buildings, the group stopped in front of a gigantic scarlet vertical slab about 100 feet long and 50 feet tall. Cream-colored streaks encircled the red rocks, making the whole ensemble look like vanilla-raspberry swirled ice cream; where there was more white, it looked like a flattened blood-shot eyeball. Anna was continually amazed at the rock structure.

Jeremy leaped atop a small boulder and started hollering and pounding his chest like Tarzan.

Anna shot back with an edge, "Hey, ape boy, lose the testosterone and let's get climbing!"

The group laughed.

"Sweet. Girl's got a bite," said Edgely. He slapped Anna a high five, then, without warning, squirted his water bottle on his dreadlocked hair and shook it like a shaggy dog, spraying Anna. His big, toothy smile flashed back and forth.

Mr. Tucker chimed in. "OK, Anna. Where do you want to climb?"

"Me?" Anna asked. "I get to choose where we climb?" She gazed at the daunting cliff, for the first time noticing how massive it really was. Straight vertical. She looked to the top and back to Jeremy. "You've got to be kidding me," she mumbled to herself. "That's impossible for me. It's sheer rock face."

"They said it was impossible to make an airplane fly," Jeremy said. "Trust me. It's possible. These are all relatively easy climbs. It's a nice beginner's spot."

The rock hovered ominously over them. Only a few nubs and cracks were available for handholds. To the right, a slab of rock jutted out from the main face, making a formation that looked like a big opened book.

"I'll give it a try, I guess."

"Good. Now, where do you want to climb?"

"How about over there?" She pointed at the opened book.

"I'll set up the ropes," said Doc McCallister. She and Jeremy scurried around the side of the cliff and scrambled their way to the top. Edgely handed Anna a harness and taught her to secure it.

"It fits kind of tight," Anna said.

"It's worse for guys, girl," one of the male students said. "Trust me." Edgely and Anna laughed.

"Rope!" came Jeremy's voice from above. A cord whipped its way down the mountain and the two ends smacked the ground.

"Jeremy and Doc just set up some anchors for the ropes," said Mr. Tucker as he grabbed the end of the line. "The middle of this rope is strung through a secure, thick aluminum ring at the top of the cliff. You'll tie into this end."

"Rope!" yelled Doc McAllister from above. Another cord zipped down the rock, the ends smacking the ground. A third rope zipped down, only this time Doc McAllister was attached to it, and she was rappelling down the cliff. She seemed to control her speed with her hand, which was holding the rope behind her. With a few bounces, she set foot on the ground. Next, Jeremy teetered over the edge, fastened himself to the rope Anna had been holding, rappelled down and touched ground right between her and Mr. Tucker.

"Good work, my man," said Mr. Tucker.

The climbers flocked to the two other ropes, excited to get climbing. In seconds, they were clinging to the rocks like gecko lizards, making progress towards the top.

"You ready?" Jeremy asked Anna. Without waiting for a response, they plopped a helmet on her head and tied one end of the rope to her harness. Anna nervously eyed the half-inch thick rope and balked, "You sure this is safe?"

"On my mother's grave," Edgely swore. "Stop stalling and let's see what you've got."

"Yeah, come on. We didn't bring you out here to play in the sand," Doc McAllister coaxed.

"Trust me," said Mr. Tucker. "You have a greater chance of being hurt on the way to the cliff than climbing it," Mr. Tucker said. "I'll even teach you the safety commands. I need you to ask me a question. You're going to ask if you are 'on belay.'" Mr. Tucker attached a device to his harness that he called an "ATC" and fed the rope through it.

"What does 'belay' mean?" Anna asked.

"Belay is the word for what I'm going to do when you are climbing. I stop the rope if you fall. You're tied into that end of the rope, then it goes through the anchors up top, and back down to me. Look, go ahead and try to pull on your end of the rope."

She did, and Mr. Tucker pulled on his end. Anna couldn't make the rope budge.

"See? If you fall, you're not going anywhere. OK?"

"If you say so," said Anna.

"When you ask me 'On belay?' you're asking if I am ready to protect you from falling."

"OK. On belay?"

"Your belay is on," said Mr. Tucker after he double-checked his knots. "Now tell me what you are doing."

"I'm climbing."

"Climb on!" said Mr. Tucker. "Everyone, Anna's doing her first climb!" A flurry of cheers erupted from the group. Those who weren't climbing or belaying turned to watch.

Anna reached up for the rock. She smeared her hands around, trying to find something to grab onto. She squeezed a decent-sized lump of sandstone with her right hand and, with some effort, found a hold for her left hand. She then lifted one of her feet, trying to use a crack for a foothold, but her toe slipped. Gravity flung her body backwards and she hung by the rope barely two feet off the ground.

"Good thing you're tied in!" Tommy Edgely joked.

Giggling a nervous laugh, Anna tried the climb again, getting no further. After three tries, Anna decided to call it quits. "I can't do this. I'm not strong enough. I'm not tall enough."

Anna's doubt set something off in Mr. Tucker. He lowered her to the ground and switched to a much more personal tone. "Listen, Anna, life is going to deal you the hand it chooses to deal. You are who you are, as you are, where you are. This is what you've been given. You now have a choice. You can complain about what you've got, sit on the pity pot, and go nowhere with your life. Or you can realize that life is yours for the taking and that you get out of life the same effort you put into it.

"Anna, it is not what happens to you that matters. It is what you do about what happens that matters, like we talked about." The group was silent as Mr. Tucker continued. "This is powerful because it means you are not a victim of life. You cannot blame your genes, your parents, or your past experiences for how you are, no matter how bad they are. You choose how you live your life every moment. It's completely up to you.

"When you realize that you are the captain of your own fate and master of your own ship, life's possibilities become endless. You decide where your life goes. You decide how your life goes. You decide why your life goes. Goals are yours to set and yours to reach.

"Your life is your responsibility. Nothing is ever achieved that stays in a dream. You've got to decide whether or not you want to climb this rock. Decide to take action!"

"I want to, but I'm not strong enough," Anna objected, a bit overwhelmed by the speeches.

"It is not your muscle holding you back. This sport is ninety percent brain, and ten percent muscle. The problem is how you are thinking. The problem is in your determination."

Edgely brought some wisdom to the table. "William James said, 'The greatest discovery of our generation is that humans can change their state of being by changing their state of mind.' For simple dudes like me, that means you can change who you are by changing how you think. Mr. Tucker is saying that you gotta want to climb so badly that you can visualize yourself doing it. Don't just think *about* climbing. Think like you *are* climbing. Believe you are doing it. Throw out your fears about how gnarly it seems. Make up your mind to climb, then climb."

Jeremy said, "Sir Edmund Hillary was the first guy to climb Mt. Everest. He's one of my heroes. He said, 'It is not the mountain we conquer, but ourselves.' Conquer yourself, Anna!"

Anna looked at Jeremy and thought about that phrase. *Come on Anna, these people all believe in you. Conquer yourself.* She closed her eyes and pictured herself climbing up the cliff, just like Tommy suggested. Everyone was quiet. For a few brief seconds, it was difficult to imagine herself climbing, but she soon saw herself pinching little nubs and cracks, sticking her footholds in the right spots, and eventually making it to the top. All the way to the top.

Anna opened her eyes. "OK, I'm ready. I'll do it. On belay?"

"Your belay is on." Mr. Tucker said.

"Climbing," Anna said.

"Climb on."

Anna made the same start up the cliff this time up and used the same foothold she had slipped on before. She pushed right up past the place she had fallen from. Hand. Hand. Foothold. Foothold. She was climbing, just like she imagined! She believed she could do it and it was happening. She was like a spider on a web. Maybe like a monkey, or a frog on the side of a glass aquarium, climbing up the cliff. Cheers of encouragement were coming from below. Looking down, she couldn't believe how high she'd come. Hand. Hand. Foothold. Foothold. Up. She was climbing! Anna realized she wasn't breathing and took a breath, smiled at herself, and finished her way to the top. "I made it!" she yelled to the people below who looked like Lego men. They burst out in applause and whistles.

"Yeah, way to go!"

"You da bomb!"

"Aaaaaw, yeeeeah!"

Looking at the horizon, she could see all of Red Rock Canyon. Rays of light beamed between the mountaintops, illuminating parts of the fiery-red iron deposits in the rock. She looked below. The group was just starting to quiet down. Anna couldn't tell what was a bigger rush: being on a vertical cliff face fifty

JOHN BEEDE

feet up or being cheered on and encouraged by the energy in this group.

Jeremy told her to lean back and put her weight on the rope. She did, a little nervously. With her feet flat on the rock and body perpendicular with the cliff, Anna's weight was completely on the anchors. Mr. Tucker lowered her to the ground and the cliff whizzed by. She touched to the ground and Jeremy gave her a big bear hug. "Nice job!"

"Thanks! Wow, that was really fun!" she told the group. Her smile was ear to ear.

"Congratulations." She slapped a hand high five and her fist bumped into two or three other fists. "Yeah!" someone gave her a quick backrub. "We knew you could do it."

"Are you off belay?" Mr. Tucker asked.

"Oh, yeah. Sorry. Off belay." Anna untied her knot.

"Belay is off," said Mr. Tucker with a grin. "Nice job. Very nice job."

The group spread out between the three ropes and Anna began climbing with the whole group, learning how to belay along with some climbing techniques. *Maybe things in Las Vegas might turn out all right after all.* By the end of the day, she was proficient at tying the necessary knots as well as belaying and putting on a harness. Most importantly, she was having a

- 49 -

ball. She particularly enjoyed Jeremy offering to belay her most of the time.

"So, how do you like climbing?" asked Jeremy

"I love it!" Anna's cheeks were sore from grinning. Laughter was a very common experience with this crowd. "Hey, I'm sorry I was a jerk earlier. I should have given you a chance."

"It's OK. We've all been there."

After everyone had climbed until they were too tired or sore to continue, they reclined for a late-afternoon lunch break. Mr. Tucker struck up a conversation with Anna.

"So, what did you think of the first lesson?" he asked.

"Lesson? I've only been climbing," Anna said.

Some of the other climbers moved closer so they could hear the conversation.

Mr. Tucker grinned. "No way, all that climbing you just did... you just learned the first lesson: *Pick a Summit.*"

"Oh, goodie. More words I don't understand," Anna said with sarcasm. "What's a summit?"

"The summit is the top of a climb or a mountain. The peak. A summit is your personal goal or destination. Essentially, it's where you want to take yourself."

Mr. Tucker continued, "The lesson applies for everything in life, Anna. You've got to pick goals. If you see a cute guy, he's your goal and you have two options. One is you can talk to him, let time do its work, and you're golden. Option two is to walk away in fear, never knowing what could have happened. The same goes for things of more significance. If you've made a goal to get into a college, you can get the grades and test scores, fill out the applications, and do your best to get accepted. Option two is to sit back and wait for them to call you. That's not likely. If you have always wanted to be an actress, that dream is nestled deep inside your heart—you have to make the choice to go after it! Hey, this goes for *anything*. If you want to be our country's first female president, you can make the goal to build your political career and put your name on the ballot, or you can sit back and wish it would happen. The moral is that you make your own experience. You choose your goals.

"There is potential within each one of us here to change the world for the better, but we've got to start with ourselves. Too many people die with their music still in them. You've got to decide if you want to let the music out, or if you want to keep it hidden.

"Anna, did you know that you were about to choose to make yourself a prisoner?"

"I was?"

"Oh yeah. You were scared to climb. You didn't have the confidence to see yourself doing it."

"It was scary!" she defended.

"You know what we climbers tell each other when we don't feel like climbing?" asked Mr. Tucker.

"What?"

"Shut up, buck up, and start climbing."

Anna laughed.

"Don't be a prisoner to your fears. Losers make excuses for why they can't do something. Losers whine and complain about their lives. Losers blame other people."

Anna didn't say anything, but she realized she had been doing all those things.

Mr. Tucker continued, "Larry Winget is an excellent author and speaker. He's got a great quote. He says, 'If your life sucks, that's because you suck.' I'd add to that, 'Winners have great lives because they are great people.' I believe winners choose where they want to go in life and they get there. You want to be a winner, right?"

"Well, yeah, of course."

"So what are you going to do?"

"I think what you're telling me is if I don't have a summit in mind, or a particular place I am trying to go, I will probably never end up getting anywhere." Anna said.

"You got it. *Pick a Summit* means to pick a goal."

"Sounds simple." She said.

The group started hollering as though they knew what was coming. "Simple is it, Miss Keller? Well then, why don't you show the group how easy it is."

Anna put on a jittery smile.

"Yeah, Anna, come on and show us!" came a voice from the climbers who were all starting to stand up and put their packs on, as though a collective brain told them where they were going. The ropes and anchors were all put in bags, and the group was soon following a steep trail up through the rock structure. They often had to use their hands to scramble over the pink and red boulders that blocked their path. Rock structures towered to either side of them, dozens of feet in the air. They continued to hike, higher and higher in elevation. Anna's legs felt like rubber, and she thought she would have to turn back several times. But she found strength from within that allowed her to continue.

The rocks abruptly ended, and the group found themselves at the top of one of Red Rock's peaks. There was a three hundred and sixty degree panoramic view showcasing both Red Rock Canyon and the city of Las Vegas. Heavenly rays of golden sunlight split the clouds like Moses parting the sea, the desert dust created a blazing red and orange sunset. Mountains in the distance cast a shadow over the valley floor. Each of the separate peaks, towering at several thousand feet, stood undaunted. It was every painter's dream sky. The city behind them was equally stunning; enormous casinos thrust themselves out from the city's blanket of houses and stores. Everyone was quiet for several minutes as they took in the beauty. *Holy smokes! I never knew the desert could be so beautiful!*

Mr. Tucker was the first to talk and got straight to the point. "OK, Anna, see that slab of rock over there?" He pointed to a slab the size of a flattened basketball.

"Yeah."

"Go flip it over."

She moved towards the rock like it was a treasure chest. Standing beside it, she looked back at the group. They gestured for her to flip it. Her sore fingers clenched a corner and overturned the stone. Anna read aloud what it said.

Pick a Summit

Don't ask yourself what the world needs. Ask yourself what makes you come alive and go do that. Because what the world needs is people who have come alive.

Mr. Tucker told her, "That's a summary of all we've said. It's by a man named Harold Whitman."

"It's beautiful."

"And true," Jeremy said.

"You've got a choice to make, Anna," said Mr. Tucker. "Do you want to keep climbing with us?"

"Yeah, I think I do," she said, a little hastily.

"Then here they are, Anna. These are your choices."

"My choices?"

"Look at the horizon. You are going to get to the top of one of these mountains. There are over a dozen to choose from. Pick one of those mountains. In time and with training, you are going to ascend the cliff you choose."

"One of *those* cliffs!? Yeah right! They're all so tall. I mean, they've got to be at least ten times the size of what we did at the Magic Bus."

"Actually, most are closer to fifteen times as high. I believe in you, Anna. Doc McAlliser and Tommy Edgely believe in you. Jeremy and the rest of the group do too. As you go through life, your challenges are going to be greater and greater, just like in climbing. You're going to need several months of training to get up whichever cliff you choose. But we're all here to support you. So, choose."

Anna looked around the canyon. Each of the climbs looked so high, yet Mr. Tucker's words of encouragement were sparkles of hope and faith sitting in her eyes. "I'll climb that one." She pointed across the canyon.

"Perfect. That's Juniper Canyon. The best climb over there is called Crimson Chrysalis. It's tough, but not the most difficult."

"You really think I can make it up that? Today is the first time I've ever been climbing, you know." Anna still doubted her mentors.

"You set a goal, Anna. That's a step the majority of people in this world never take. But you have set this goal—to reach the summit of Crimson Chrysalis—and you're going to do it with our help. Trust us.

"For now, though, I get to assign your first and only homework assignment. I want you to write out twenty-five of your life goals. Pick summits that you think would make you come alive. Things you'd really like to do. They can be short term, long term, things you've always wanted to do, things you suddenly realize you'd like to do. I want to see twenty-five of them. Write them down and bring them to me by Wednesday.

"Twenty-five? I don't think I can…"

"Stop right there. Most people don't think they can come up with 25 goals because they've forgotten how to dream. Can you remember when you were a kid and everything seemed possible? That's how I want you to treat this. With the excitement of a child. How are you going to know what your dreams are unless you take the time to truly dream about them? Twenty-five it is. Most of the people who never physically write their goals down don't achieve them. Ever. So I'll see the list by Wednesday?"

"Yeah, sure, I guess. But could you tell me how I'm going to do this Crimson Chrysalis?" Anna asked.

Mr. Tucker and Jeremy both pointed to Edgely, who was sitting between them, chewing on a granola bar. "That's the next lesson!" He answered with food in his mouth.

1. Pick a Summit.

- The world needs only people who have come alive. Find what makes you come alive and go do that.

- Once you've decided what makes you come alive, that is your summit.

- Remember, you are the master of your fate and captain of your ship. Whatever you want to do, you can do.

- Losers make excuses why they can't. Winners figure out how they can.

- It is not the mountain you conquer, but yourself. Conquer your fears.

Application:

Turn to page 124 of this book and write out twenty-five goals (use your own paper if this is a school or library book). Not just a few goals… twenty-five. Work on it over a few days and add as many goals as you can think of. If it comes to mind, write it down! Dream like you did when you were a child. (Author's note: I'm dead serious about this. Get them on paper. Don't be a lazy bum. Take control of your life. Put your pen and paper to use. We're going to be using your goals throughout the book.)

CHAPTER FIVE

Notepads and Coffee Cups – Sunday Morning

Anna smacked the snooze on her 5:00 AM alarm. She had forgotten to reset it from yesterday morning. 5:09 AM. Snooze. 5:18 AM. Snooze. In her sleepy daze, she finally figured out how to turn off the clock. A few hours later, she flopped out of bed and onto the ground. *Oh, man I'm sore!* Anna dragged herself up off the floor and fragments of yesterday's memories started flooding back to her. She massaged her forearms as she thought about what she had learned. She recalled Jeremy's words from last Friday as well. "It does not take a complicated idea to transform your life. It takes a simple idea that you decide to apply to yourself." That stuck out to her. *Apply to yourself.* Anna saw the connection. *I've got to figure out how to apply these concepts to my own life. It's no good just knowing them. I've got to do something about what I learn...*

Still in her pajamas, she went into her dad's office and took one of his legal-size yellow notepads. He had stacks of them in the closet. Anna sat at her desk and wrote at the top of the page, "*My Summits,*" listed numbers one through 25, and began dreaming about everything she was remotely interested in doing with her life, one goal at a time. She made it up to goal number 13 and called it quits. Some of her favorites were, "Visit Australia," "Get along with my family," "Write a magazine article," and "Get at least a 'B' average when I graduate."

What can I do right now to start changing? "Get along with my family" stuck out to her. *Dad. He's probably downstairs, alone, reading the paper. I haven't had a good talk with him for a long time now. No, this is stupid. Well, I can't even remember the last talk we had that wasn't a fight. Things used to be so good between us. I think he still cares. We've just lost our connection.*

Hey, I choose my life's course. I can make things better with my dad or I can let them get worse. Anna rolled her chair out from her desk and decided to go talk with her pop. She hesitated one more time as she stood at the top of the stairs. *He's my dad. I want a better relationship with him. I should just make it happen! I choose my own experience.* Stepping down the stairs, she looked at her father reading the paper, coffee mug in hand. She stood on the third stair, directly in front of him. He hadn't noticed her yet.

"Dad?"

He looked up, fully attentive. "Yes, Anna?"

"We...Dad...umm...I guess...I just miss being with you, Dad. I miss you."

Slowly, Anna's dad lowered his newspaper, resting it on the table. "You feeling OK?"

"Yeah, I was just thinking we hadn't talked in a while. I miss you."

He stood and walked right towards Anna with his arms extended. Her eyes welled with tears and they embraced. "I miss you, Anna," he said. "I've missed you too."

They got Charlie, and with arms on each other's shoulders, the three of them strolled down the block for ice cream sundaes at a local shop.

* * * * *

Aron Ralston

Conversation was lively. Anna had forgotten how funny her dad was. He had become more solemn after the divorce, so it was refreshing to see the playful side of him again.

Soon, her dad was telling her about a story of a climber he saw in a few TV interviews.

"His name was Aron Ralston, and while he was hiking in a canyon, a big boulder fell on his arm, pinning him to the floor. He was stuck for six days when he finally intentionally broke his arm and amputated it with a dull Leatherman pocket knife."

Anna's little brother cringed.

"What amazed me was that he said he has tried more activities after the accident than he did before, like bareback horseback riding. The best part is that he continues to climb mountains. All with a prosthetic arm! He also said that he appreciates his family and relationships more than he ever would have if the accident didn't happen."

"He picked his *Summits,*" Anna whispered.

"What?" her dad asked.

"Aron. He set goals for himself. It's what I learned yesterday. He didn't let what happened to him stop him from living life to the fullest. He decided to choose his life! All these things he did were goals he set for himself. He didn't let his accident get in the way. That's what it means to *Pick a Summit!*"

Anna's dad eyed her in a way that was half-proud, half-confused. "Sounds like you're learning more than just rock climbing out there."

"Yeah, I'm learning about life," she said as she scooped the last bit of vanilla ice cream in her mouth and scraped the chocolate off the side of the cup.

CHAPTER SIX

Fighters and
Colored Pencils – Monday

The next morning, Jeremy picked up Anna for school and they talked about climbing. Anna gave him a hug before heading off to class.

Between her third and fourth hour classes, Anna was at her locker and noticed one of the guys who was in the fight last Thursday. It was the dark haired guy who kicked the brute on top of her. He was cleaning out his locker.

Anna started, "Hi. Anything I can do for ya?"

"No." He faked a smile. He hadn't even looked up, let alone noticed she was the girl he'd clobbered.

"You sure you don't want me to carry some of your stuff? I've got an extra arm and…"

"What's your problem?" He looked up at Anna with steely eyes. "I don't want your help. Wait. Aren't you…"

"The girl you wasted when you kicked that guy on top of me?" Anna answered for him. "Yeah. That's me."

"Oh. Sorry 'bout that. Well, if it makes you feel better, I won't be around 'cuz I got suspended for fighting. Something about a 'cool down period.' I guess I can come back Wednesday. Whatever."

"Sorry to hear that," Anna said. She went back to her locker, only a few spaces down from his. She turned her combination, grabbed her books, and was about to go to class, but had a feeling this guy needed some help. *I make the choice here. I can forgive him or hold a grudge.* Pulling out a piece of paper and some colored pencils, she quickly made a card that said,

Look forward to seeing you back at school!
Luv, Anna

She held it out to the fighter. "Here you go!" she said. He looked at the note, then at Anna.

He didn't say a word.

Anna smiled. "I made that for you. And hey, don't worry about what happened. You didn't mean to. Well, see ya!" Before he could say anything she slipped off to class so she wouldn't be late.

*   *   *   *   *

The Human Brain

White lab coat. Glasses. Tie. Very thick Italian accent. Mr. Finochario was Anna's eccentric psychology teacher. White hair. Wrinkles. He could have passed for Einstein. As usual, he started class with a bizarre statement that sucked the classroom into his weird world of science: "Students, the Russians used to cut people's heads up. Did you know that? They believed they could determine what makes a person great by examining the brains of their greatest leaders and thinkers. You know what they found?"

The room was silent.

"Nothing! Ha! Ha ha!" Mr. Finochario threw his hands in the air, spun around, and sat down on his desk. He was an odd cookie, no doubt. But a smart odd cookie.

"You see, my students, every human mind has great potential. It does not matter where people come from or what race they are," he continued. "The latest findings in anthropology, sociology, psychology, and physiology show that the potential of the human mind is very great indeed." His eyes widened. Anna tried to figure out which "-ology" was which. "Man only uses a small part of his brain. If we could use just half of our full capacity, the average person could easily learn 40 languages, memorize the *Encyclopedia Britannica* from cover to cover, and complete the required courses from every university and college in America. The possibilities are endless."

The teacher was bubbling with delight at his knowledge. The class stared blankly, as usual.

"My children, does anyone know what this means for you?"

He drove his students nuts but calling them "my children." They gave him silence again.

"It means," Finochario broke into song and waved his hands like he was orchestrating a symphony, "you have plenty of room in your brains to study for the chapter test this Friday!"

"No! Boo! Come on, Mr. F," the students grumbled.

Normally, Anna would have joined in. However, she was thinking about what Mr. Finochario said about the capacity of humans. Mr. Tucker wasn't messing around.

If my brain has the capacity to learn so much, that means I have to decide what to put in it. I am responsible for my life. I bet I can score pretty high on this test if I really try to.

Life Note

At the end of the day, Anna went to her locker again. A folded note had been stuffed inside. Scribbled on the outside was,

From Chris

Chris... Chris... who is Chris? She slowly unfolded the note and another paper fell out of it. She read what was on the inside the note.

Anna,

Sorry again about knocking that guy on you. Anyway, because of the note you gave me earlier today, I decided I don't need this anymore. It's a page I ripped out of my journal. I guess there's life on this planet after all. Thanks, and see ya.

Chris.

It was from the dark-haired guy whom she had given the card to. The fighter!

She reached to the ground, grabbed the journal page, and found a much darker topic inside. Phrases like "life's just not worth it anymore," and "it hurts too much" littered the entry. Towards the end, a few sentences caught her eye.

"I've been thinking a lot about dying lately. I wonder... if I killed myself, would anyone notice? Does anyone really care?"

It hit her what had happened. *Chris decided suicide isn't worth it because I showed him I care.*

She leaned against her locker and covered her mouth with her hand, loosely holding the note in her hand. She may have *saved a life* that day because she made the choice to make the best of a bad situation that was thrown her way. *Amazing. It really does work.*

Celebration

Jeremy came looking for Anna. She hadn't come to his car as planned and he got worried. Anna explained the whole story, and they hugged.

"Hey, let's go talk to Mr. Tucker about this. He'll probably be able to help more," Jeremy said.

They strolled into Mr. Tucker's office. He was finishing his day with the paperwork he loved to put off.

"Hey! Look at these awesome people!" Mr. Tucker was his friendly self. "Come in. Sit down."

Anna related the events that had occurred since they went climbing Saturday, including how she sat down to write out her goals and about her day with her dad.

Mr. Tucker paused a moment after Anna was finished speaking. "People normally take weeks and months before the lessons start to really sink in, Anna. This is amazing. You've done a wonderful thing."

"He's right, Anna," said Jeremy, "If everyone put these lessons to use like you have, there'd be an incredible change in a lot of people's lives."

"Wait. Before we talk about climbing and success strategies, I want to make sure that you aren't going to call Chris or his family and betray my trust with him. That wouldn't be cool at all."

"Don't worry," said Mr. Tucker. "Whatever is said between us is confidential. But I am going to need to work with you in order to help him. I'd like to counsel him when the time is right." Mr. Tucker knew that thoughts of suicide recur if not properly treated.

"Good. That sounds good, Mr. Tucker. Just let me know what you want me to do."

The three of them agreed that if Chris was interested, they'd bring him to Red Rock to learn to *Climb On!*

"Hey, how are those twenty-five goals coming?"

"I'm up to thirteen," Anna said back. "But to be honest, I kinda want to learn the next lesson, if that's OK." If the first strategy alone could bring this much good to her life, she wanted to make even more happen.

"Finish those goals by Wednesday, like we talked about. You'll learn soon enough."

Anna pulled her list of summits out of her bag and wrote, "Help Chris get better," and "Get an 'A' on Finochario's test."

"What are you doing?" asked Jeremy.

"Making sure I'll be ready for Wednesday," she said.

CHAPTER SEVEN

Tommy Edgely's – Wednesday

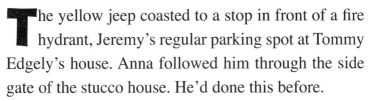

The yellow jeep coasted to a stop in front of a fire hydrant, Jeremy's regular parking spot at Tommy Edgely's house. Anna followed him through the side gate of the stucco house. He'd done this before.

When they came around the corner, Anna saw why Jeremy would want to come over. It was incredible. Half the yard was an artificial climbing wall, about twelve feet tall. It wrapped and twisted across the width of the yard. Overhanging caves, flat sections, and cracks gave a home for hundreds of multi-colored, goofy-shaped holds bolted to the spotted gray surface. There were a few surrounding palm trees to give the structure shade.

"I can't believe this is someone's backyard," Anna said.

"He's a stuntman. Of course he's got a cool back-yard."

"Whatever. This place is nuts!"

Jeremy knocked on the sliding glass back door. A pretty woman slid the door open, started to say something, but was interrupted by two little boys, barely older than toddlers, bolting out the door like monsters, both snatching onto Jeremy's legs.

"Jeremy! Jeremy! Walk!"

The two brothers plopped themselves on Jeremy's feet. He stampeded them around the yard, leaving Anna at the back door.

"You must be Anna?" the woman asked. Anna nodded. "I'm Tom's wife, Joyce. Tom!" She yelled into the house. "He'll be right out. Can I get you something to drink?"

"No, thank you."

Edgely emerged, removing his glasses. It looked like he was studying, which was weird, taking his dreadlocks and piercings into account.

"Yo, my main woman Anna! Sup, playa?"

"Hi, Mr. Edgely. How are you?"

"Chillin' like a villain." Anna saw his wife roll her eyes. "Outta here like Vladimir. Haulin' like Stalin. Makin' time like Frankenstein. What's goin' on? You meet my kids?"

"Yeah, looks like Jeremy's just started Wrestlemania Nine with them." All three were rolling in the grass. "I'm here to learn the next *Climb On!* lesson, I guess."

"Oh, for sure." He laughed with his usual toothy grin. "Come on, then, let's do some climbing." Edgely trotted to the enormous climbing structure, pinched a mold of an orange smiley face and hung from it. He gestured for Anna to hop on the wall. They were about three feet off the ground. "Watch how awesome my kids are," Edgely said as he winked at Anna. "Mark, Luke, Daddy's falling! Ahhh! Get Daddy a crash pad!" The boys and Jeremy ran around the back of the wall and emerged moments later with a giant foam mattress. They slid it under Anna and Edgely. "Can't…hold…on…anymore…" With that, he fell backwards onto the cushions of the mattress and was enveloped in the foam. "Oh, you guys saved my life, I thought I was a goner for sure."

"Daddy, you're silly," one of them said.

"I know," he said as he stood up. "Now go run in and help your mommy with dishes, OK?"

"Blah! Dishes! Blah!" they chanted as they ran into the house, leaving Jeremy, Anna, and the stuntman all smiling.

"They're cute," said Anna, still hanging on the wall.

"I love 'em," said the stuntman. "OK, so, climb around. Let's chat." He and Jeremy both hopped on the wall and started making moves. Anna followed in suit. "You want to learn the next lesson, eh?"

"That's the idea," she said as she lunged for a hold that looked exactly like a banana.

"Well, that depends on your homework. Did you do it?" He grunted, slipped, and fell onto the crash pad. "Nuts. I can never make that move."

"Yes, I did it."

"Awesome" Edgely said, getting off the crash pad. "Let's see 'em."

Anna climbed a few feet to the ground and pulled her goal sheet out of her pocket. "One through 25, here you go."

Edgely read each of the goals, one by one. "Sweet. Sweet. Gnarly. Cool." He finished the list. "Righteous work. Yeah, great work. Do you think you'll be able to do all of these, Anna?"

"I think with enough time I can."

"You're right. With enough time, you can definitely do everything. I see here you've got 'Get a degree.' I also see 'Backpack around Europe.' Both are wicked goals, right? But both of those take time, though? You can't do all of it at once."

Anna looked at Jeremy, still on the wall. He was smiling a knowing smile, listening.

"Writing these goals out, whoah, sweet move on your part. Bet it's one of the top ten best things you've ever done for yourself, but you've got to accomplish them in bite-sized pieces. So we gotta figure out what's most important to you." Edgely went to his shed, grabbed a felt tip marker, and handed it to Anna. "Cross out any goals that are not yours."

"What do you mean? They're all mine." She scanned the list again.

"Take some time to think about this. Think about what's really *from you*. If you don't truly want to do something you wrote down, but only wrote it because someone else expects you to do that, or has, like, put pressure on you to reach that goal, cross it out."

"Can you give an example?"

"For sure. Jeremy had a goal to get certified as a Coast Guard captain." Jeremy nodded. "After he thought about it, he realized it wasn't his goal at all. No! It was his dad's goal for him. If you have anything like that listed, I want you to cross it out. You may have a bunch or you may have just a few. So, give it a try."

"Yeah, OK, I can do that."

She took a few minutes and crossed out three of her twenty-five goals. "Own a business," which was something her mother always wanted to do, "Get a model portfolio taken," which was something her friends from Colorado always encouraged her to do, and "Visit Canada," were all crossed out. She had no idea why she put that on the list.

She passed the marker and list to the Edgely. "For some people, what you crossed out are fantastic goals," he said. "For you, though, they aren't what you really want to do, right?"

"Right." Anna was surprised to see how much other people had influenced her.

Now, I want you to take a look at that list, and ask yourself, "Are these going to hurt anyone?" If so, I want you to cross them out. I don't know if you've got anything on there that will or not, but, if so, not cool."

"Tell the Eskimo story," Jeremy said. He was now reclined on the crash pad.

"Oh yeah, I almost forgot. So, Anna, do you know how to hunt wolves in the tundra?"

"I have no idea."

"All right, so, certain Eskimos take a sharp, double-edged knife, dip it in seal blood, then freeze the blood around the blade. You follow? They dip it again, and re-freeze the new layer. Over and over this process goes until it's like a Popsicle of seal blood with a knife as the stick in the middle. Crazy, eh?" Anna cringed. Edgely continued, "To kill the wolf, they bury the knife handle in the snow. That way, the frozen blood is sticking straight up into the air. Now, to wolves, seal blood is the tastiest thing around. It's their pizza. Their steak and potatoes. Their biscuits and gravy. So they come by, lick it, and the warmth of their mouth melts the frozen blood. And they love the taste so they keep licking, and they think it's like, so righteous. Free seal blood! But sooner or later, they reach the knife and cut their own tongue. But because they are so focused on getting pleasure out of the situation, they ignore the pain and they lick the bare knife until their faces are so mangled that they bleed to death."

"That's disgusting," Anna said.

"You're right, it is. What's even more disgusting is that there are people all around you who do the exact same thing every day. People are so focused on getting physical pleasure, thinking it will lead to happiness, that they ignore the pain they are doing to themselves and to other people. So many people die physically from overdose or suicide or bulimia, or whatever else. But most people… most simply let the life they were meant to live—a life of goodness—die. Like the wolves, people in this world try to satisfy their hunger with bogus "food" and end up worse off because of it."

"So, take a look at your list. Is there anything that is going to hurt anyone else? I want you to cross it off. Better yet, if you can, change it so you make the situation better.

While he was talking, Anna felt convicted. Number 17. "Get even with my mom." She took her pen and painfully drew a line through it. Edgely didn't say anything. She looked down at the page again, knowing what she had to do. She wrote in its place, with even more pain than the cross-out took, "Forgive my mom." The stuntman sensed she was done. "Sweet action. Now, cross out all but the most important ten goals on your list."

"What? I want to do everything here," Anna protested.

"I understand. But when you cross a goal out, you aren't saying that you'll never do the goal; you're saying that it's not as important as another and can wait until later. For now, focus on your most important goals so that you can actually accomplish them and not spread your efforts thin. Then, after you accomplish one, you can add another."

"Well, how do I decide?"

"Couple ways. You can ask yourself if your goal is realistic, for starters."

Jeremy spoke from the crash pad, "I had a goal that said I was going to make a million dollars by the time I turned 21. I got rid of it because it wasn't very realistic."

"There you go," Edgely said. "You can also ask yourself, 'Can I commit to this?' I've always wanted to climb Mt. Everest, right? But I've got a wife and kids, and my stunt show, and they all need me alive, right? So it'd be messed up if I went and died on them. I take risks but they're all very calculated.

"But really, it's going to come down to what's in your heart. What's really important to you? So, you work on that and I'm going to work on this climbing move."

Anna grabbed the marker back and started thinking about her goals. It took her about fifteen minutes to complete the process. She was defining success for herself.

She ended up with the following:

1. Help all people, however I can.
2. Forgive my mom for what she did to the family.
3. Get my high school diploma with a 'B' average.
4. Stay physically fit (and not use drugs or alcohol).
5. Get a degree from a good college.
6. Find a part-time job.
7. Visit 20 foreign countries in my lifetime.
8. Learn to play the guitar.
9. Climb Crimson Chrysalis.
10. Help Chris get through the Climb On! lessons.

"Done," she said, and passed the new list to Edgely.

"These are totally wicked, Anna." He looked over them again. "Yeah, way sweet.

"Some of these are what I call *destination* goals, and others are *journey* goals. Destination goals are cool because you can know when you've reached your *Summit*. When they hand you your diploma, you'll know you've arrived at your *Summit*. But a journey goal is something, like, to stay physically fit. These are things that you can never put your foot down and claim, 'I have now arrived at my goal. I am a fit woman, hear me roar.'" He smiled. "They are ongoing and take constant work. Every day you gotta work at journey goals.

"The last step is to make an action plan for your goals. Check it out!" He walked over to a shed and gestured for Anna and Jeremy to follow. They did.

"So, one of your goals was to climb Chrysalis, eh? Well, let's figure that out." He pulled on a hanging string that popped a bare light bulb on. It illuminated a room that looked like the motherload of all climbing gear. There were ropes everywhere. A giant bag of harnesses sat on the floor. Funky metal blocks and nuts were hanging from the walls. To keep dry hands while climbing, an entire shelf was devoted to chalk and chalk bags. It was insane.

So let's get this monster figured out!" He dove right into the gear. "You're gonna need about six quickdraws," he said as he flung them at Anna to catch. "One-two-three-four-five-six! Probably three sets of big gear and maybe a medium set, eh, Jeremy?" Jeremy nodded and the stuntman pitched the gear at them both. A harness, climbing shoes, chalk bag, and two water bottles all came flying, along with some other gear, most of which Anna had no idea what it did. She and Jeremy stood like rotted Christmas trees, metal hanging from every limb.

"So, this is what you do with your goals, once you have your top ten list. You scope out three last things: Who's gonna help you? How do you prepare? And what's the action plan? How are you going to climb Chrysalis?"

Anna answered, "You're going to help me. I prepare by climbing every weekend, maybe more over here, or at the gym, and probably learn how to use this gear, and the plan is...climb it?"

They laughed. Jeremy said, "We're going to study a map of the climb, figure out when to use which gear, and yes, then we go climb."

"Hey Anna, guess what?" asked Edgely.

"What?"

"You just learned the next lesson, *Gear Up!*"

They all said it together. "Sweet."

"Let's do some more climbing!" Anna said.

2. Gear Up!

Decide what your most im-
portant goals are and create an
action plan to reach them.

Application:

Take your list of 25 goals and do three
things.

1. For each of your goals, ask yourself,
   "Is this right? Is it what I want?" If not,
   cross it out. "Is this going to hurt anyone?" If
   so, cross it out. "Is this doable and can I commit
   to this?" If not, cross it out.

2. Cross out all but your ten most important goals.
   For each one, ask yourself, "Is this goal realistic
   and can I really commit to reaching it?" Follow
   your heart on this one.

3. For each goal, make an action plan. Who is going
   to help you? How will you prepare? What's your
   course?

Congratulations! You've just defined what success
is for yourself. Post your list on your mirror or on
the inside of your door so you can remind yourself
of your goals every day.

*Author's note: It will be very tempting to skip this pro-
cess. DON'T! If you figure out your most important
goals and write them down, your chances of being successful are much greater than if you don't. Trust me!*

CHAPTER EIGHT

Personal Summits – Wednesday Evening

After greeting her dad and telling him about her day, Anna grabbed a snack and went upstairs to begin studying for her Psychology test. She ran through Edgely's questions. *Is it right? Of course. Even though other people want it too, it's also what I want. It's definitely not going to hurt anyone. It's good too. It'll help me. OK, check on the first question.*

Is it do-able? Well, I've never been too hot at Psych. I think I can reach this if I work hard enough. Can I really commit? Yes. I'm doing it right now. What's in my way? I've got to learn all of chapter 12.

So, last question, what's my plan? There's tonight, tomorrow, then test day. If I study tonight and tomorrow and review Friday morning… hey! That's only nine pages a day. Shoot, I can do that. That's the plan, then. I'll go get help from Finochario after school tomorrow as well.

She cracked the dusty text and began working through her nine pages. Anna also decided to learn chapter vocabulary and to review class notes. A few times, she found herself thinking of Jeremy or wanting to go downstairs to get a snack. *Nope, I've got to keep on track.* She stuck her head back into the book. After only about an hour and fifteen minutes, she finished her reading and she knew the vocab well. *All right! That wasn't so bad after all.*

Palm Valley Developments – Thursday

Anna slipped into her first class a few seconds after the bell rang. Her teacher gave her a look of disapproval as they stood for the Pledge of Allegiance. Morning announcements followed.

Anna made the regular stop at her locker between third and fourth hour classes. Chris was just closing his locker as she arrived.

He was nervous when she approached. "Hey, I don't want you to think I'm some sort of freak or something like that," Chris said. "I mean, I'm just having some tough times and want to get away from everything. So don't think I'm whacked out."

"No, no, it's cool, Chris. I understand," she said. It wasn't too long ago that she was sitting on her rooftop wishing the pain would stop as well. "I've had some rough spots too. We friends?" Anna held out her hand.

Chris took her hand. "Sure, I guess."

"What was so bad anyway?" asked Anna.

He nervously twisted his foot on the ground like he was squishing a cockroach. "I, uh…things are tough with my family. It's just really hard."

Anna understood his reservations. "It's OK. I understand." She reached forward and put her hand on his shoulder in support

"Ahhhh! Ouch!" Chris squirmed and struggled to escape her grasp. Anna dropped her arm immediately. Chris's shirt was pulled to the side in the scuffle and Anna couldn't help but notice a large bruise on his neck that curled around his shoulder.

He stood several feet away. "See? Family problems." He pulled his shirt back over the bruise. "Like I said, it's tough at home."

Anna was reminded of when her little brother, Charlie, was abused. Chris's case looked worse. "Hey Chris?" she asked. The two of them still stood staring at each other.

"Yeah?"

"Wanna go rock climbing with me and some of my friends this Saturday?"

"What do you mean?"

"Every Saturday, we go rock climbing. I just learned last weekend. It's really fun. Anyway, I want you to come this Saturday."

"I've never been," he said.

"So why not give it a try?"

"I've always thought it looked cool on ESPN."

"So you'll come?" Anna persisted.

"It sounds OK."

"I'll take that as a yes."

Anna got Chris's number and promised to call Friday afternoon with details.

After school, Anna spent 20 minutes with Finochario, studying the concepts she didn't yet understand, then she met Jeremy in the regular parking spot. A gentle wind jostled his sun-bleached hair. *He is so cute!* Anna thought to herself. The more time she spent with him, the more she liked him. Jeremy seemed a little nervous. They got into his jeep without saying much to each other.

"Why so quiet?" Anna prodded.

"Huh? Oh, nothing."

"Nothing? Nothing is never nothing," Anna teased. "Nothing is always something, and something is what keeps people quiet. You have something you want to say?" Anna was getting to know Jeremy pretty well by now.

"Sort of."

"Well then, why don't you, duh, sort of tell me?" Anna teased.

"Anna, it's nothing I want to tell you. It's something I want to ask you." Anna was quiet. "I think you are an amazing person. You intrigue me. You have a magnetic, no, an enchanting spunk to your personality and you're unbelievably beautiful. I care for you a lot and would like to take you out tomorrow night."

Anna was flattered and blurted out, "Well, isn't this convenient? It just so happens that I'd love for you to take me out tomorrow night."

Jeremy reached across the seat and gently locked fingers with Anna.

Test Time – Friday

Anna turned over the paper and read the first question, which asked, "This is the gray exterior of the brain that transmits impulses and messages to various parts of the brain." *I know this one! It's the "cerebral cortex." Answer B.* On the entire test, there were only a few questions about which she was unsure. For those, the process of elimination helped knock out the bad answer choices. She double-checked her answers. Deep breath. She stood, walked to the front of the class, handed in her test and waited for the rest of the class to finish.

When everyone was done, Mr. Finochario said, "OK, you wait here. I use Scantron machine, OK?" When he got excited, his English worsened. Grading Scantrons was the sort of thing that excited Mr. Finochario.

He arrived back in class just in time to catch a guy throwing a spitball. The eccentric professor scolded him: "You'd be beat with stick if you went to school I went to!" He handed out the graded tests after his tirade.

In faded red ink, Anna read her test score. *Ninety-two?! A ninety-two percent! That's an A minus! I beat my goal! I did it!* Anna was gleaming on the inside. She wanted to scream at the top of her lungs. Life was coming together.

After school, Jeremy drove her home. "We still on for tonight?" He asked.

"Of course. I didn't forget!" Anna said.

Anna told her dad and brother about the test. "Well, this deserves some celebration!" Anna's dad said. "Ice cream for everyone!" He reached into the freezer for the vanilla, grabbed three bananas, and concocted three of his famous banana splits.

After the celebration, Anna called Chris and got directions to his house so they could take him climbing the next day. "OK, I'll see you at 7:30," Anna confirmed. "Can't believe I'm doing this," Chris said.

"You're gonna love it. Trust me."

Later that day, Anna and Jeremy celebrated Anna's successes at her favorite restaurant, The Spaghetti Factory. Afterwards, they raced go-carts, which turned into a game of bumper cars. Laughing hysterically, they got kicked off the go-cart track, so they tried min-iature golf. They lost their golf balls in the waterfall, which made them laugh even harder.

At the end of the night, Jeremy walked Anna to her door and she kissed him on the cheek. "Thanks, Jeremy, I had a wonderful time." Jeremy paused a mo-ment then shuffled his foot uncomfortably.

"Anna May, I have to go." He said abruptly. "Sorry. Uh, see you tomorrow morning." Jeremy rushed back to his car and drove off. Anna watched from the door-step then slipped inside.

CHAPTER NINE

The Black Corridor – Saturday

Anna's alarm clock screamed like a bottle rocket. *I've gotta get a radio alarm.* She got out of bed, gathered her stuff, blitzed out the front door, and hopped in Jeremy's jeep without using the car's door. They picked up Chris, who immediately hit it off well with Jeremy because of his CD collection. The yellow jeep followed the lonely, one lane road to Red Rock Canyon, the desert sunrise as its background.

The group of climbers were the first people of the day to arrive at the duly named Black Corridor. Two walls separated by a blanket of sand rose from the corridor floor fifty or sixty feet into the air; their black streaked faces stared at each other.

On the way into the thin corridor, Edgely strapped on his helmet and piped up, "Welcome to the Black Corridor, everyone. Please keep your hands and feet inside the vehicle at all times!"

Doc McAllister smacked the back of his helmet. "You're a kook."

"Is that your final diagnosis, Doctor?" Edgely mocked.

Everyone was used to their goofiness except Chris.

"They play like this all the time. You'll get used to it," Anna warned him.

"Whatever," Chris shrugged.

The climbing began and Chris went with Mr. Tucker while Anna raced Jeremy to a cliff top. She was amazed at how she could glide up the rock, nearly effortlessly this time around.

At the top of the cliff, Jeremy asked, "Anna, why don't you try some of the harder routes with me?"

"Sounds good to me." They started descending and Jeremy pointed up the corridor.

"There's a climb over here called 'Dancin' With a God.' I've got to lead climb these routes which is a tad different than what we've been doing. At the Magic Bus Wall, we stationed ropes at the top of a climb, which is called top-roping. Here, there is no way to walk around and set up anchors, so as I climb, I've got to clip the rope into those bolts. Other climbers drilled them in every six or ten feet up the cliff, see 'em?"

Anna squinted and saw small, shiny metal hangars on the wall.

"Yeah, there they are."

They touched ground and began untying their ropes.

Jeremy continued. "It's also more dangerous this way because if I fall, I fall double however far I have climbed above my last bolt."

"I don't get it."

"Say I'm four feet above my last bolt. I fall four feet to the bolt, then another four feet below the bolt, until the rope goes taught."

"You could fall eight feet?"

"Once I fell twenty when I was ten feet above a bolt. Hurt like nuthin' else."

"You sure this is safe?"

"I fell because I wasn't climbing smart. I skipped a bolt because I got cocky. Anyway, you'll be fine because you're gonna climb after me, so after I climb the rope up and set it in the anchors, you won't be able to fall more than 6 inches."

"OK."

They moved a few feet up the corridor, roped up, and Jeremy began his climb as Edgely belayed. Jeremy clipped the rope into the first bolt with a device called a 'quickdraw,' consisting of two carabiners and a piece of webbing connecting them. He trotted past five more bolts on the climb, veins and muscles bulging, and tied into the anchors at the top.

"Your turn!" he yelled from above.

Anna lowered him, they traded gear, and she started climbing. She quickly saw why Jeremy's muscles were bulging. She was pinching nubs with nothing more than the pads of her fingers, sometimes less than that! Her shoes slipped and smudged on the rock face as she clumsily muscled her path. She climbed about fifteen feet up.

"I don't know Jeremy. This is pretty tough."

"Just try and…"

She fell with a quick shout. Her body whipped and hung by the rope, inches from her last climb spot.

"OK, now I'm freaked out." Anna said. Jeremy tried to reassure her.

"Grab the wall; see if you can get back on."

She reached from her suspension point and pulled her body towards the cliff.

"OK?"

"Go for it," Jeremy said from below, a little more concerned than he was when they started.

She started climbing again; her arm muscles started shaking. Her forearms pounded. She had hardly moved five feet and was stuck, this time with a sharp edge jabbing her right index finger.

"Ahhh! I can't hold on. Falling!" "I gotcha!"

Anna fell again, her hair fluttering everywhere until she was caught by the rope. She visualized, tried again, and fell. She talked herself through it, tried again, and fell. She fell, over and over.

"Let me down. I can't."

Jeremy fed the rope through his hand, and lowered her to the ground, where Doc McAllister had shown up to watch.

"You did fine," she said.

"I couldn't do it." Anna looked up at the cliff. "There's nothing to grab onto."

"Jeremy, can you give us a moment?" Doc asked in her classic English accent.

"Sure. I'll be down with everyone else. You'll get it Anna, don't worry."

He walked down the corridor while Doc and Anna took a seat.

"Let me tell you a story," Doc said. "I read it in TIME Magazine a few years back.

Maisie DeVore

"In the small town of Eskridge, Kansas, Maisie DeVore had an official day named after her— July 14—to honor the realization of her dream. Her *Summit*. Thirty years before this particular day, Maisie saw the need for a community swimming pool. The small town didn't have the budget for a pool, so Maisie vowed to come up with the money by collecting aluminum cans. She collected hundreds of thousands of cans over the thirty years that she had her *Summit* in front of her. As Maisie's goal received more attention, funds came in from other sources. A grant from the Kansas Wildlife and Parks came through. A movie celebrity donated funds. After three decades of collecting money, primarily through collecting cans, Maisie had the $200,000 necessary to complete the project. Construction began in April. In the middle of July, Maisie had ascended her summit and the pool was opened to the public thirty years after Maisie set her goal.

"That's unbelievable! She paid for a pool with cans? Holy smokes!" Anna was duly impressed. "That's the beauty of the *Climb On!* philosophy, Anna. The unbelievable becomes believable. Most people would never believe they had the ability to climb fifty feet into the air, let alone the fifteen hundred you are going to climb at Crimson Chrysalis, which is a lot harder than this climb." She was looking straight at Anna.

"Harder? I'm never going to do that. I bailed on this one. No way."

"It seems impossible to earn two hundred thousand dollars from cans, but it happened because Maisie DeVore decided to *Ascend It!*"

"Huh?"

"The process of going up a climb is called the 'ascent.' So, after you *Pick a Summit* and *Gear Up*, you do the actual climbing. You *Ascend It!*"

"I'm listening."

"It's the same thing you are going to do with your summit, Crimson Chrysalis, and hopefully with any other goal you set for yourself."

Anna was ready for specifics. "OK. How do I do it?"

Doc McAllister picked up a stick and wrote in the dirt.

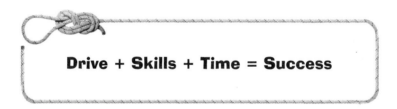

Drive + Skills + Time = Success

"To reach the *Summit* of Crimson Chrysalis, or to reach the *Summit* of any goal you set for yourself, you simply follow this formula: Drive + Skills + Time = Success. Let's take them one at a time.

"Drive comes first. Just how badly do you want it? Drive asks whether or not you are going to do what it takes to reach your *Summit*. The choice is yours.

"When climbers ascend Mt. Everest, they sometimes have to hike past dead bodies left on the mountain. They literally have to look death in the face to reach their

- 97 -

goal. They spend months at the base of the cliff, acclimating to the altitude, fighting the weather, and waiting for it to give them a good day to climb. That's drive.

"Skills comes next. When someone has the desire to do something without having the skills to do it, it makes for a bad combination."

"A wanna-be!" interrupted Anna. Doc chuckled.

"Actually, you're right. If you want to do something but don't have the skills to do it, you become a 'wanna-be.' So, you need to develop the right skills to reach your *Summit*. For climbing, these skills are strength, endurance, balance, and mental persistence. Over the next few weeks and months, we will be working on developing these skills with you, and we'll take you up the climb once your skills are ready. In other goals, the skills it takes to succeed will differ. For example, if you want to get straight A's, there's not much physical skill needed, but your brain skill has to be top notch." Doc McAllister tapped her temple with her index finger.

"So how do I develop these skills?" Anna asked.

"Some people say practice makes perfect. Well, sorry to burst the bubble, but that's a lie."

Anna took a swig from her water bottle and didn't interrupt. Doc was confident and continued.

"Practice does not make perfect. *Perfect practice makes perfect.* If you practice making mistakes, you're only getting better at making mistakes! You develop the skills to reach your *Summit* when you have plenty of the right kind of experience. You like basketball?"

"I dunno."

"A coach of a University basketball team used to say that 'the will to win is nothing without the will to prepare to win.' I believe he is right. Your goals can be entirely beyond your abilities…and that's perfectly OK, as long as you take the time to perfectly practice the skills it takes to reach that summit."

"That makes sense," said Anna, "I've got to learn the right skills in addition to having the drive to succeed."

"The last part of the formula is time. You can't throw an egg in a barnyard and expect it to crow to-morrow."

Anna's dimples leapt two inches up her cheeks. She liked that analogy.

"It takes time to develop skills, Anna. Sometimes it takes time to develop sufficient drive. Sometimes time just means waiting until the right moment to do something. If you're a basketball player and you want to average fifteen points a game, that's a very do-able goal, but it will probably take more than an entire season of practice to make it happen. More often than simply waiting, however, the 'time' part of the formula means getting up each time you fall. It means persisting like a marathon runner.

"For example, a lady was walking along a street in France and she spotted her favorite artist. It was Pablo Picasso himself! The lady was bold enough to approach the great artist and ask him to paint her portrait. He agreed, and she sat down for the fifteen minutes it took Picasso to paint her. 'That will be fifteen thousand francs,' Picasso announced as he flipped the painting around for her to see. The portrait was a masterpiece, but the lady was shocked at the price. 'Fifteen *thousand? That only took fifteen minutes!*' she protested. 'No, Madame,' Picasso said, 'It took me a lifetime.'

"You see, Anna, Picasso knew it took him *years* to reach his level of artistic skill, and he charged accordingly. Success takes time, either way you look at it.

"Next to Hank Aaron, do you know who has the record for the most homeruns in baseball?"

"Babe Ruth, right?"

"Yes. Do you know who has the second most strikeouts?"

"Nope."

"Babe Ruth. He struck out 1,330 times. You see, great people who accomplish great things always have to persist at their goal over time, and sometimes that means failing. There is no such thing as an overnight success. Michael Jordan was cut from his high school basketball team. He could have given up after that setback. But he knew basketball takes drive, skills, and time, so he stuck with it, and now he's known as the greatest basketball player of all time."

Anna added to the conversation, "I think I understand. I read this thing that said airplanes are only facing directly toward their destination city for two percent of their flight. The other 98 percent of the time they are off course because of turbulence, other planes, the wind, and all the other factors. But the pilot knows exactly where he or she is going and because of little corrections, the plane arrives at the city. I guess each destination is like a *Summit,* and it just takes time to get there…plus a very skilled pilot." Anna laughed. "And I sure hope you have a pilot who has enough drive to take you to your destination! Wouldn't that be weird if the pilot just gave up in mid-flight? Would he announce that on the intercom, 'Well, folks, this is your captain speaking. I know you want to go to Chicago, but I think I'm just going to land in this here Iowa cornfield. I don't feel like going the rest of the way. You all have legs, so why don't you walk.'"

Doc laughed.

"You're a funny girl, Anna. Well, that's all for *Ascend It!* Do you have any questions?"

"Yes, what about talent? Doesn't talent come into the picture?"

Doc thought for a second. "People everywhere want to know if they have enough talent to succeed. It makes me sick, like they're waiting for success to fall into their lap or hoping Santa Claus will drop it off in their stocking. People seem to think talent is like frequent flyer miles—collect enough points and you can redeem them for a free trip. I say bullocks to that. You have enough raw talent for *anything*...just as you are. Everyone does. It's what you are born with. You cannot escape the natural talent you've been given. It's just a part of who you are.

"This is not to say that everyone can be a superstar at anything they want. Sure, talent plays into the picture in the cases of highly skilled experts, but on the other hand, some people who are bursting at the seams with raw talent have gone nowhere because they never refine their talent and develop the right skills it takes to succeed. I know many people who are much more talented climbers than I, but I can whip their hineys on the rock because I've developed my skills over time with my drive to succeed. Talent itself is never enough to succeed.

"I like how President Calvin Coolidge put it. He said, 'Press on. Nothing in the world can take the place of persistence. Talent will not; nothing is more common than unsuccessful men with talent. Genius will not; unrewarded genius is almost a proverb. Education alone will not; the world is full of educated derelicts. Persistence and determination alone are omnipotent.'"

"I never thought of it that way," Anna said.

"Glad to shake things up in that skull of yours. Come on, let's go climb with everyone else. You can come back to this climb some other day."

They met up with Chris, Mr. Tucker, and the others. Soon the group was hiking up to the same spot where Anna found the "Pick a Summit" rock. It was Chris' turn to learn the same lesson. He seemed to be challenged by it as much as she was.

Jeremy, oddly enough, decided not to join the group on the hike, complaining of a headache. He went with Edgely back to the cars.

The group finished their day climbing and hiked back to the parking lot, enjoying the stunning sunset and laughing. They met up with Edgely and Jeremy, cruised home, and before long, Anna plopped down on her bed and was sleeping like a rock.

3. Ascend It!

- To reach your *Summit*, you *Ascend It!*

- Success is made by combining Drive + Skills + Time.

- Be like Picasso and measure your worth by the *years*!

- Get up every time you fall and keep on moving.

- Practice doesn't make perfect. Perfect practice makes perfect.

- Talent is not nearly as important as your desire to succeed.

Application:

Start following your plan to accomplish your goals. Stick with it. Persist. It may take a lot more hard work than you initially thought, but with enough stick-to-it-iveness, you can make it happen. Once you reach your summit, celebrate your accomplishment.

CHAPTER TEN

Murphy's Law – Sunday Morning

"Hello?" Anna answered the phone groggily, just waking up.

"Anna?"

"Yeah, who's this?"

"Anna, its Mr. Tucker. You need to get to Sunrise Hospital."

"What happened?"

"It's Jeremy."

"What? Oh no, Mr. Tucker, tell me what's going on."

"He's very sick. Can you get a ride?"

"Yeah, I'll be there soon."

Anna woke her dad up and they went to the hospital together and found Jeremy's room. Mr. Tucker was outside with Edgely and Doc. Anna's mind clawed, each scenario she could think of worse than the last.

"Anna," Mr. Tucker started, "Do you remember when we first talked in my office?"

"Yeah…" She was getting even more nervous.

"I told you there was someone at school who was very sick. With HIV."

"Oh, no. Please say it's not him—is it?"

"Yes. It's Jeremy." Two nurses walked past. The walls seemed to get closer. "His grandparents are in there now, but he wants to speak with you when you're ready."

Anna started to cry, still not believing what was happening. Her mentors left her alone and spoke with her dad.

She swung the door open, and saw him there on the bed.

"Anna May Keller. Why are you crying every time I see you?"

She smiled through watery eyes. "Hi Jeremy," she managed to get out.

"Sorry I didn't tell you. I didn't want you to look at me differently. Hey guys," he said to his grandparents, "This is Anna. Anna, my family. Could you give us some time?"

They filed out of the room.

"So there were these complications, blah, blah, blah. But I get all the pudding I want, so it's a nice trade-off."

She smiled through her pain, again. "Oh, Jeremy."

"So I bet you're wondering what the deal is. Well, there's no use lying about it. Um… I've made some really poor choices. Really bad ones. I can try to blame it on my parents who practically abandoned me, or blame my situation. I can point lots of fingers, but it just comes down to some bad decisions I made. That's it."

"That doesn't seem at all like you." Anna said.

"It's not anymore. When I found out I was sick, I realized I needed to change who I was. After my depression I took up climbing and I was healthy enough to do that and go to school. I wanted to. So I did. Now I can't."

"You must be so upset. This is a nightmare." Anna thought she sounded petty.

"I've gotten used to the meds and the doctors and all the problems. But yeah, it's pretty serious this time. My immune system weakened at a faster rate than usual, and they're saying I may have some other illness because of that or that it could possibly be AIDS. They're still doing their tests."

Anna stayed with Jeremy for the long, painful day. After long hours of conversation, nurses, needles, machines, and doctors, he fell asleep. Anna snuck out of the room and went home to sleep in her own bed.

*   *   *   *   *

Grace – One Week Later

"You been climbing?" Jeremy asked, spooning vanilla pudding into his mouth.

"Nah," Anna said back. They sat alone in the hospital room.

"Whaddya mean, nah? Why not?"

"It's just not the same without you there."

"It was never about me, Anna. It was about you feeling better about yourself and life."

"I'm so upset that this is happening to you. I can't concentrate. I can't think. It's so terrible. I want to scream. I can't function. I know I haven't known you long, but you mean so much to me."

"You mean a lot to me too, Anna."

"So, if this is what the world is gonna give you, me, us, I say it's not worth it."

"Stop right there. Haven't you learned anything? You're just going to give up on all your goals? Everything you worked so hard for you're turning your back on?"

"I feel like I hate so much right now. I was right when I said life sucks, then you…" She didn't want to finish the sentence.

"Die?" Jeremy finished for her.

"Yeah."

"Anna, I've gone through all the anger and hatred

for everyone and everything under the sun. And nothing good came from it. I'm not mad at my condition, or life, or the world, or anyone. Even my parents. "

"You should be."

"Listen to me." She didn't respond. "Anna, listen." She turned her head away. "Edgely and Mr. Tucker have given me some books to read while I've been boxed up in here. I marked some of the parts I liked."

He grabbed at one of the books and read a quote. "William Arthur Ward: 'Forgiveness is the key that unlocks the door of resentment and the handcuffs of hate. It is a power that breaks the chains of bitterness and the shackles of the selfish.'" Anna looked back at Jeremy. "When I read that, it stopped me dead in my tracks. I wrote next to it, in the margin, 'Forgiveness is a virtue found by few and exercised by even fewer, yet within it lies the power to bring kingdoms to their knees and the potency to transform vicious hatred to unfailing love.'"

Anna said, "Jeremy, that's really beautiful. You're so amazing."

"I want you to really think about what I'm saying, Anna. Listen to these other things I found." He flipped to a page with a bent corner. "Here it is. Gandhi said, "An eye for an eye makes the whole world blind." I believe he's right. Somewhere else in here I read that after the Civil War, Abraham Lincoln was urged by his advisors and other politicians to punish the South for all the havoc and deaths the war caused. Lincoln said, 'Do I not destroy my enemies when I make them my friends?' Forgiveness could very well be the sole reason America exists today."

"Jeremy, where are you going with all this?"

"Anna, I want you to forgive the world for all of this happening. I want you to forgive your mom, too, like you said you would at Edgely's."

Anna looked away for a few moments. "She doesn't deserve to be forgiven."

"It's not about what your mom deserves. It's about what you deserve. You deserve to forgive her so that you can be free from the bitterness and hatred that you have. She's already caused so many of your family problems. What makes you think it's fair for her to make you feel so much hatred? The only way to get rid of your own self-destructive anger is to forgive her. Show her grace."

"What do you mean?"

"Grace is love applied. It says, 'I love you' without any strings attached. Grace says, 'Regardless of how you hurt me, I will still love you.' It says, 'Where you fall short, I will cover the remainder of the distance for you.' Anna, grace is a gift. If you want to forgive your mom, you must give her grace. I know you love her; otherwise she wouldn't have had the capability to hurt you so badly. I'm sure at times you thought you hated your mother for what she did, but you shouldn't have to be crippled by that hatred."

Anna nodded. "This isn't about me and my mom. You're the one who's sick."

"Don't change the subject. I've loved my life the last few years. I'm happy. I find so much joy in everything. My body is sick, sure, but you and everyone out there who don't really live their lives…they're the ones who are ill. My character is not sick. So, yes, this is about you, because you're the one with the worse disease.

"My suggestion, Anna, is that you take those intense feelings you have for your mother and channel them to create grace rather than hate."

Anna wrestled with whether or not she would be able to do that.

"In this book by Phillip Yancey, *What's So Amazing About Grace?*, there's a news story about a bomb that exploded amid a group of protestants in Ireland. Eleven people were killed and over sixty wounded. Caught beneath five feet of debris were Gordon Wilson and Marie, his twenty-year-old daughter. Marie's last words were, "Daddy, I love you very much." She died in the hospital a few hours later. Gordon Wilson survived the attack and soon the press was printing stories about him and his daughter.

"Wilson said, 'I have lost my daughter, but I bear no grudge. Bitter talk is not going to bring Marie Wilson back to life. I shall pray tonight and every night, that God will forgive them.'

"'The world wept,' said one reporter, when he told the story over the BBC radio.

"Upon his release, Wilson led a crusade for Protestant-Catholic reconciliation. Protestant extremists who had planned a counter-bombing decided such actions would be foolish because of the publicity surrounding Wilson. The Irish Republic eventually made Wilson a member of its Senate. In his book, Wilson constantly repeated the refrain, 'Love is the bottom line.'

"It's the same with your mother, Anna. Love is the bottom line. Do yourself a favor. Do her a favor. Love her. Show her grace. Forgive her."

Later that day, Anna phoned her mother. "I love you mom," she confessed, "and that's the bottom line."

EPILOGUE

The Crimson Chrysalis – Several Months Later

Anna sat with Chris and Mr. Tucker on a ledge they estimated was over eight hundred feet in the air. They were on the last "pitch," or stretch of rock, until they reached the top of the Crimson Chrysalis. During the last several months, Anna's life had been very busy, but she remained happy. School finished in early June and Anna ended up with a 3.1 GPA for the semester, which she brought up from a 1.9 at the quarter. More than the grade, however, she was proud that she had applied herself. She knew she had given it her best effort. Her parents couldn't be more pleased.

Despite the success, Anna was glad school was done. During the summer, she'd trained for the summit of Crimson Chrysalis at the local climbing gym several times a week and faithfully joined the climbing group each Saturday. She had learned a horde of climbing wisdom, tactical skills, tricks and tips, and ways to safely climb to greater heights.

She visited Jeremy in the hospital almost every day. On Sundays, she stayed nearly the whole day. Jeremy's health continued to decline as he struggled through the pain and became increasingly embarrassed of the lesions. He was too sick to climb and sometimes too ill to stand, but he'd always be there, impressing the doctors with his overall strength given the circumstances. And asking for more pudding.

Now, here Anna was, ascending her personal *Summit* with Chris and Mr. Tucker. She looked down the cliff. The only thing separating her from ground below was eight hundred feet of air. *Cool.* A bead of sweat dropped from her brow…and plunged…and fell…until it was out of sight. Perhaps it evaporated in the summer heat.

Making sure all was secure, Anna started the commands.

"On belay?"

"Your belay is on."

"Climbing!"

"Climb on*!*"

Up Anna went, pinching hand-holds she couldn't have dreamed possible a year ago. She jammed her climbing shoes into the small vertical crack that directed the climb. Hands covered in chalk to prevent sweat from gathering, fingers wrapped with athletic tape to support her joints, her body danced up the cliff like a spider on its web. A poet would be in awe. Every so often, she'd take a moment to plot out her next few moves, then do them, lead climbing the *Summit* she had picked so many months before. Her drive was so intense that the hairs on her neck stood on end. Or was that from the chill of the wind at eight hundred feet in the air? She had the skills. The last few months were sufficient time for them to develop. She ascended, arm over arm, foothold after foothold. The sandstone passed by as she pranced up the climb, graceful as a feather in the wind. Her aching hands latched onto a big horn-shaped rock and she pulled herself up onto a ledge. She stood up straight and looked around. This was no ledge at all. This was the summit. She was at the peak of Crimson Chrysalis. Anna had learned to *Climb On!*

She let out a holler of excitement, the noise echoing off of the canyon walls. Chris and Mr. Tucker followed her lead. Soon, the three were at the top, standing side by side, awestruck at the view.

"You did it, girl!" Mr. Tucker congratulated as he took a seat on a rock. "Congratulations."

"Thanks Mr. Tucker," Anna said graciously.

"Yeah, good job," Chris said.

"Chris, I think that's the first nice thing you've ever said to me," Anna said.

Mr. Tucker jumped in, "Yeah, that's impressive, Chris. I didn't think you knew how to talk."

Chris defended himself, "Hey now, you're a teacher, you're not allowed to make jokes."

"Counselor, Chris. I'm a counselor," Mr. Tucker asserted.

"Whatever you say, old man," Chris jabbed.

The *Climb On!* philosophy had made Chris change his attitude for the most part. He was still battling depression and constant family issues, but was coming around in his own timing and enjoying climbing. That's the beauty of the strategies. They work for anybody, no matter where they'd like to go with their life.

"Mr. Tucker?" Anna started. "Something doesn't seem quite right."

"What do you mean?"

"Well, lessons are a great thing, but they don't seem to be...I don't know...complete."

"That's because you don't have the full lesson," Mr. Tucker said without flinching. Both Chris and Anna turned their heads in bewilderment. "What?!" they said in unison.

"You are lacking one lesson." Mr. Tucker stuck his hand down under a rock and pulled out a faded tootsie roll wrapper another climber had left on the mountain peak. He held it up, showing them. "There's a lot of trash in this world. Countries are at war. AIDS and cancer are ripping lives apart all over the world, as we know too well. If next week is typical, 200 people your age will die in car accidents. Another 155 will be murdered. About 90 will kill themselves. Your parents' divorce rates are off the charts. People are lost in despair, hurting, lonely, and afraid. This world has a lot of trash in it.

"When I was in Boy Scouts, they taught me something I didn't appreciate at the time, but it means a whole lot to me now."

"What was it?" Anna asked.

"They taught me to leave every place you go better than you found it. Compared with how long the earth has been here, humans are only a wisp of smoke, really. We're just passing through, that's all. The way I see it, you have three choices. One: you can leave the world better than you found it. Two: you can leave the trash where it is. Or three: you can make the problem worse. I say it's up to us to clean up the trash. Someone who has truly learned to *Climb On!* leaves the world better than they found it. This is why I am a counselor, why Edgely teaches these lessons, and why Doc McAllister is a doctor. These are the ways we have chosen to help the world. Aharon David Gordon once said, 'We must enhance the light, not fight the darkness.' I think Jeremy would like that."

"I do too," Anna said.

"Chris objected, "Hold on. This makes no sense. Why wasn't the world just created or made with no problems? How come there is so much pain in the world? Everywhere I look there's people hurting, including me."

Mr. Tucker started right into a story. "A man walked past a cripple and a beggar and a beaten woman. And seeing them, he looked to the sky. In great pain, he cried out, asking the same question you just asked, 'How is it that the world can possess such things and yet do nothing about them?' Out of the long silence, the man finally heard the earth's answer. 'I did do something. I made you.'"

Silence. All three climbers reflected on the story. The wind softly whistled through the cracks of the red sandstone and blew against Anna's cheek. It reminded her of Jeremy's kiss. Mr. Tucker spoke first. "Jeremy helped you, Anna, because he knew this lesson. He was making the world better in his own way. You're now doing the same for Chris. You see, you both have the ability to reflect the light that you have been given and leave this world better than you found it."

They packed up their meals and began to rappel down the hundreds of feet they had just climbed. Something about the descent reminded Anna of the time she climbed down from her roof the first time she and Jeremy met. Her transformation had come full circle.

Anna put the *Climb On!* philosophy to get what she truly wanted out of life. It worked for her.

It will work for you.

Climb On!

4. Leave It Better Than You Found It

- You have three choices. One: you can leave the world better than you found it. Two: you can do nothing about the world's problems. Or three: you can make the problems worse. Choose wisely.

- Don't forgive your enemies because they deserve it. Forgive them because you deserve it.

Application:

- Forgive your enemies and wrongdoers. Forgiveness is a virtue found by few and exercised by even fewer, yet within it lies the power to bring kingdoms to their knees and the potency to transform vicious hatred to unfailing love.

- Remember Gordon Wilson's statement, "Love is the bottom line."

- Reflect the light you have been given. Teach the *Climb On!* strategies to another so that they can also set goals that will improve the lives of other people.

The Climb On! Strategies for Success

1. Pick a Summit

2. Gear Up

3. Ascend It

4. Leave It Better Than You Found It

ABOUT JOHN BEEDE

* * * * *

John has nothing short of a passionate love for worldwide adventures. He has ridden elephants in Thailand, explored penguin colonies in South America, Muy Thai kick-boxed with world champions, been  scuba diving with whale sharks, whitewater rafted off of waterfalls and through caves lit by glowworms, and much, much more.

And, of course, there's the rock climbing. About 30 minutes from his Las Vegas home is Red Rock Canyon, home to a staggering number of world-class climbs. John has also climbed on 5 continents and has reached the top of dozens of the tallest peaks in North America.

A select few of his planned future adventures are to climb the '7 Summits' (the tallest mountain on all 7 continents), sail around the world, snowboard through a flock of penguins in Antarctica, become trilingual, backpack the Great Wall of China, and to start a string of self-sustained charity projects at the worldwide locations he visits.

John welcomes correspondence from his readers.

BIBLIOGRAPHY

* * * * *

The author recommends and thanks the following resources:

Christensen, John, Stephen C. Lundin, and Harry Paul. *Fish! A Remarkable Way to Boost Morale and Improve Results*. New York: Hyperion, 2000.

Covey, Sean. *Seven Habits of Highly Effective Teens*. New York: A Fireside Book by Simon and Schuster, 1998.

Covey, Stephen R. *Seven Habits of Highly Effective People*. New York: A Fireside Book by Simon and Schuster, 1990.

Cutler, Howard C., and Dalai Lama. *The Art of Happiness: A Handbook for Living*. New York: Riverhead Books, 1998.

Krakauer, John. *Into Thin Air*. New York: First Anchor Books, 1999.

Maisie's Community Swimming Pool. DeVore Community Swimming Pool Association. <http://maisiespool.com>.

Peale, Norman V. *The Power of Positive Living*. New York: Ballantine Books, 1990.

Ralston, Aron. *Between A Rock and a Hard Place*. New York: Atria, 2004.

Swain, Todd. *Red Rocks Select*. Evergreen, CO: Chockstone Press, 1995.

Tracy, Brian. *21 Secrets to Success*. CD. Topics Entertainment, 2002.

Winget, Larry. Speech. www.larrywinget.com

Yancey, Philip. *What's So Amazing About Grace?* Grand Rapids: Zondervan, 1997.

Ziglar, Zig. *Over the Top*. Nashville, Atlanta, London, Vancouver: Thomas Nelson, 1997

Every effort was made to attribute proper credit to this book's sources and inspirations. In addition to these named sources, however, I must give credit to the untold thousands of books, audio programs, speakers, teachers, and characters who have influenced my writing. This story and characters in this book are fictional. Any similarities to real life people or events are strictly coincidental.

APPENDIX A:
TEEN RESOURCES

* * * * *

Please visit the following websites. Each offers unique information related to this book:

www.climbonsuccess.com
The author's business website with information related to this book, John's speaking availability, and his rock climbing adventures. Free success e-course available.

www.johnbeede.com
John Beede's online journal detailing his personal adventures, including video, pictures, and multimedia.

www.ted.com
A massive collection of media composed by some of the finest minds and motivational heroes of today. MP3, video, and podcast downloads.

www.fastweb.com
The largest online scholarship resource offering massive amounts of financial aid every year.

www.teenagehealthfreak.org
Want to know if you're normal? This superb website should give you the answer to any health question you have.

The following are the websites of many youth organizations that are near you (in alphabetical order):

www.4-h.org – Has the mission of engaging youth to reach their fullest potential while advancing the field of youth development.
www.deca.org – Teen marketing, management, and entrepreneurship organization.
www.dfyit.org – Drug Free Youth in Town
www.fbla-pbl.org – Future Business Leaders of America
www.fccla.com – Family, Career, and Community Leaders of America
www.ffa.org – Future Farmers of America (Agricultural Education)
www.nasc.us – National Associations of Student Councils
www.skillsUSA.org – SkillsUSA – Trade, technical, and service organization.

National Youth Crisis Hotline: 1-800-448-4663

APPENDIX B

* * * * *

My 25 Goals Worksheet:

1.

2.

3.

4.

5.

6.

7.

8.

9.

10.

11.

12.

13.

14.

15.

16.

17.

18.

19.

20.

21.

22.

23.

24.

25.

My Top Ten Goals:

1.

2.

3.

4.

5.

6.

7.

8.

9.

10.

Be sure to create an action plan for each of your goals.

ACKNOWLEDGMENTS

* * * * *

As stubborn as I am, and as much as I think I can do everything myself, many people were great supporters in making this book a reality. They are:

My family, Dad, Mom, Mike, Jenny, Laura, and Willy. You've been my biggest inspirations my whole life. I love you.

My mentors, Scott Ginger, Kevin Tucker, Thomas Edgely, Daniel McAllister, and James Malinchak.

Gregg Storwick and Peter Self, thanks for letting me fail my way forward.

Nathan Whitmore and Chris Martinez, thanks for putting up with my 3AM typing in that awful dorm room.

Elizabeth (Rubie) Gosnell and Minette Piper, thanks for keeping me awake during my cross-country drives, for putting up with my bad jokes, and of course, Lizzie, for editing this thing.

Jim and Barb Weems, thanks for the fantastic design and layout. Well done!

Thanks to all the people who have laughed at my dreams, discouraged me, and made fun of me. Without you, I wouldn't have had the determination to finish this.

My greatest friends and mentors over the years have been all the students who have let me teach and mentor them. Thank you all.

Pass On *Climb On!*

To order more copies and see our other products, please visit **www.climbonsuccess.com**, or order using this form.

❑ YES, I'd like to order _____ copies of *Climb On! Success Strategies for Teens.*

❑ YES, I am interested in having John Beede come to my school, conference, meeting, or organization to give a workshop or speech. Please send me information.

❑ YES, I am interested in having John Beede teach a group of teens how to rock climb. Please send me information.

Please send this form plus $15 for each book to the address below. Include $4.00 S&H for one book and $2.00 S&H for each additional book. Nevada residents must include applicable sales tax.

My check or money order for $ _____ is enclosed.

Please charge my   ❑ Visa   ❑ MasterCard   ❑ American Express

Name _____

Organization _____

Address _____

City/State/Zip _____

Phone _____ Email _____

Card # _____

Exp. Date _____ Signature _____

Call 1-800-CLIMB-ON

Make checks payable and remit to:
John Beede International, Inc.
PO Box 232395
Las Vegas, NV 89105